ROBERT PORTNER KOEHLER

# STEPS TO MURDER

A DETECTIVE NOVEL CLASSIC

NOVEL SELECTIONS, INC.
NEW YORK

## *Chapter* I

I HAD practically forgotten that Joan Craig existed. It's funny how you can grow up with people, on terms of friendliness that amounts almost to intimacy, and then suddenly drop them completely from your recollections. It had been that way between Joan and myself. She was like a shadowy ghost in the memories of my childhood, and she had no place in the present, no little corner in the world in which I could picture her, grown now, a mother probably—certainly my age, which is near enough thirty to permit me to let it go at that.

I can't pretend, of course, that I ever liked her particularly. But our families had been inseparable in those days, and I knew her, I suppose, as well as I did anybody. She was always a curious, insincere person, from the days when I, in a coronet of pigtails and a stiff pink taffeta dress, and with braces on my teeth, watched her across the floor at Miss Falcon's dancing class and envied her dark beauty. She never had an awkward age, and at fourteen I resented that with an intensity that appalls me now.

She had a coming-out that dwarfed every other that season, and made the rest of us feel like the neglected refugees from an orphan's home. Her family, the Craigs, had money, and they allowed Joan to dress several years older than her age and use lipstick when Mother would have soundly spanked me if I'd tried to copy her. Later, when she eloped with Frank Murdock, father would refer to her as the prize example of the insidious effect of make-up. Candidly, even I had to admit he had something there.

That elopement shook our staid New England circle to its roots. The Craigs had practically settled it in their own minds that she would marry Thorne Emory, who was first vice-president of a bank, and eminently respectable as to antecedents. He was older than Joan, but not too much so. He might have been, people thought, a steadying influence.

And then, astonishingly, she went to an Army-Navy football game with Frank Murdock, and detoured, afterwards, by way of Elkton, Maryland, and a Justice of the Peace. She turned up on her father's doorstep a few days later, frightened but unrepentant, with Frank beside her.

He was devastatingly handsome, a tall, dark man with a small moustache, and the large, friendly eye of a collie. You could not blame Joan for being dazzled. Everyone was, after ten minutes in his company. But he simply didn't belong in our set. That sounds snobbish, I suppose, and I would only make it worse by adding that he had no family background, and absolutely no income. His brother, I believe, supported him, and James Murdock made his money—what little he had—out of editing a racing paper. There was more than that, however, to Frank's ineligibility. There was about him too much of the odor of race tracks and speak-easies, and too large a pinch of the spice of strange bedrooms.

The Craigs were horrified. You couldn't blame them, I suppose, for assuming that it was Joan's bank book, as much as her beauty, that had attracted Frank. There was talk of an annulment, but it died down, and the couple moved into a tiny apartment and tried to live on what James supplied, what Joan could wangle out of her sister, and the temporary jobs Frank managed to hold for perhaps four months at a time.

None of us ever knew if they were happy. We assumed, of course, that they couldn't be, and the birth of Joan's daughter a year later didn't help. When her parents died, Joan's share of the estate was left, in trust, to the child. Frank couldn't touch it, and that arrangement increased the difficulties.

Frank finally took a job in the oil fields of Texas, and Joan remained at home, explaining that Frank considered the oil towns too tough for her and the baby. Everyone suspected a trial separation, of course, but Joan herself denied any such rumors emphatically. But several years passed without a sign of Frank, and most of us decided she had seen the last of him.

I moved to California about that time, and Joan dropped out of my life completely. She was not the kind to write letters, and even my Christmas cards brought no exchange. Somehow she faded out of sight, and I would probably never have thought of her again if she hadn't turned up unexpectedly last spring.

I had moved into Beverly Hills, into a small house on Bedford Drive, and Web, my brother, and his wife were living in the Brentwood house, having returned from their honeymoon in Honolulu just in time to miss Pearl Harbor. The new house wasn't completely furnished—in fact, I wonder if it will ever be, what with my weakness for auctions and reshuffling furniture.

But I was adding a touch here and there; and on this particular day I was buying a lamp for the living-room.

It was a magnificent April day, without a cloud in the sky, and air fresh-washed from the sea. I came out of the shop, and saw a huge Rolls Royce parked at the curb. It was an especially refulgent model, and it had magnificent tires, such as we were beginning to envy, what with war-time restrictions. It was the tires that attracted my attention first of all, and only after my mouth had watered a little, comparing them with my own worn treads, that I saw the woman sitting in it. She was busy, typically, putting on lipstick, and at first she didn't notice me.

But I had recognized her with a start of surprise. Ten years had not changed her a bit, except to put a sort of bloom upon her. Though I knew she was thirty-two, she looked about twenty-five, with the clear, fresh skin of a child. She was small, with an impish face and humorous dark eyes. Her hair, elaborately groomed, was raven black, and she wore an outfit that went with the Rolls Royce—expensive and showy.

I leaned in the window of the car and called her name.

"Joan, of all people! What in the world are you doing in Beverly Hills?"

"Isabel!" she exclaimed, and she seemed genuinely delighted to see me. "Hop in and let me drop you somewhere. The chauffeur will be here in a minute."

"Thanks, but my own car's just down the block," I protested. "But it is good to see you, Joan. For heaven's sake, though, have you struck oil? I never would have recognized you if I hadn't seen you using that lipstick."

"Really," she said, "isn't it just too amazing? Me, the poor little outcast! Oh, Isabel, I want to tell you all about it!"

"I want to hear it. Are you staying here, or just visiting?"

"I'm living in Bel-Air," she announced. "I've got a house there for the summer. You must come over to see me. I've got so much to talk over with you. It's been years since I saw you."

"I know," I said, with a sudden guilty feeling. The last time I had been East I had neglected to look her up, and my conscience bothered me—a little. "I've become a confirmed Californian these last few years."

"Why not drop out for dinner on Tuesday?" she suggested suddenly. "Please do, Isabel. I want to explain so much to you."

That seemed an odd thing for her to say. I felt, for a moment, as if something must be bothering her conscience too, and I wondered fleetingly what it could be.

"I'd love to come," I assured her. "Where is your house?"

She gave me the address, and I told her my own.

"I'll expect you at eight," she said, "unless I call you. But Tuesday is open, I know."

Her chauffeur came just then, and I stepped away from so much magnificence, and allowed his green-clad grandeur to insert itself into the driver's seat. Joan waved a gloved hand as they backed away from the curb, and I found myself wondering frantically what I could possibly wear to that dinner that wouldn't be completely eclipsed by Joan's own wardrobe.

I must have stood on the sidewalk for some time, with a perplexed expression on my face, for two or three people passed and looked at me oddly. But I was burning with curiosity to know what had happened to her, and to Frank. I had avoided mentioning him out of possibly misguided tact, and she had not helped me a bit.

I was so preoccupied with my thoughts that for a moment I didn't even notice the man standing across the street and staring fiercely at the departing car. He stood so close to the curb that he was almost hidden by the parked cars there, but I recognized him quickly enough. It was Frank Murdock, and his face had a hunted look that not even the distance of the intervening street could blur. I stared at him, more perplexed than ever. Something certainly was wrong, and I suddenly had a strong urge to avoid him until I understood the situation a little better.

I ducked back into the shop, therefore, with the excuse of verifying the price of a lamp I had looked at. But for some reason, I had an uneasy feeling in the small of my back.

## Chapter II

Now I do not believe that I am any more of a gossip than the average woman. I do like to know what my friends are doing, and to understand their troubles and their good fortune, but I consider that purely neighborliness.

My curiosity concerning Joan was intense, just then, and Tuesday seemed a long time to wait for enlightenment. It occurred to me that Alice Trent might know something about it. It would be better, I felt, to arrive at that dinner a little prepared for Joan's disclosures, and Alice would surely have an inkling of them if anybody had. Alice had moved West only a short time before, and of all my older friends, had kept closest touch with the people at home.

Her house was only a block or two away, and when I had cautiously looked up and down the street to be sure Frank had vanished, I drove over to call.

She was in slacks under an awning on her patio. A tall Scotch and soda stood on a table beside her, when the maid ushered me out, and she greeted me effusively.

"Gladys, bring Miss Marsh a Scotch," she ordered at once. "Isabel, how nice! Sit down and tell me all the news."

"I've been buying lamps," I said, settling down in a huge deck chair. "I hear priorities may start a scarcity. You look comfortable."

"I am. I just came back from the Red Cross class, and I'm exhausted."

"I saw Joan Craig as I was coming out of the shop," I said casually. "I didn't know she was in town. Did you?"

"Joan? My dear, no!" She looked at me with what I suppose she thought was a significant look. "I wonder if Frank knows."

"He does. He was watching her from across the street as she drove off, in a Rolls Royce as long as a Pullman car."

Alice's eyes were troubled-looking.

"Oh, I hope——" she began, and fell to sudden silence as Gladys emerged into the patio with my Scotch. We both waited self-consciously until she had gone.

"Alice," I said, "what *is* going on there? Joan asked me to dinner Tuesday, and I don't want to put my foot in it when I see her. Do you know what's happened?"

"A little," she admitted vaguely. She was looking out across the patio toward the gay border of nasturtiums along the garage. I had a feeling that she was trying to make up her mind how much to tell me, and how much to omit.

"When did you see Joan last?" she asked.

"Oh, years ago. A year or two after Frank went to Texas."

"You didn't know, then, that Frank came back, did you?"

"No.'"

She nodded. "He did. He stayed awhile, and went off to some other place—Venezuela, I think. He'd come back every now and then, stay awhile, and drift off again. People wondered what Joan lived on in the meantime. And when she went out once or twice wearing a gorgeous diamond bracelet, people began to talk. It was rather indiscreet."

Alice took a long drink of her Scotch. She was a tall woman, with a lovely figure, and thick auburn air. Her voice was low and rich, the sort that appeals particularly to men, I believe.

"I don't understand," I said lamely. "Bracelet?"

"Frank wasn't nearly rich enough to afford it, Isabel. And Thorne Emory kept calling when he was away."

"Alice! That was unwise of her, if that's true."

"Oh, it's true all right," said Alice firmly. "Don't forget I was around there at the time. Once or twice I tried to say something about it to Joan. Just a hint, you know, of the impression she was making. But you know Joan."

She sighed, and set her glass down.

"Really, Joan can be the most perverse person!" she said irritably. "Strong-willed. You know. She seems to have an idea no one else could possibly have a grain of sense or ever be right about anything. Well, I don't suppose any of us were surprised when she finally picked up and went to Reno. Heaven knows I wanted to give her the benefit of the doubt, Isabel, but you know what they say about smoke and fire, and that divorce smoked like a bad chimney.

"Frank was away somewhere at the time, as usual, and it seemed that Thorne Emory had persuaded her finally to go, and he—well, he financed it.

"Of course everybody simply buzzed with tales after that. Most of them blamed Frank, but some of us, who knew Joan, wondered whether she hadn't grown a little tired of living like a pauper and was considering her own comforts without thinking much about Frank or trying to help him make a go of it. It was the sort of situation where it was almost too easy to take sides, and perhaps be unjust unless you knew all the facts. Frankly, I didn't."

She looked reflectively at the ice in her glass for a moment.

"I'm only telling you all this, Isabel," she explained, "so, if

you do see her Tuesday, you'll be prepared. I got some of the
rest of it from Thorne himself."

"Thorne Emory?" I asked. "When did you see him?"

"About a month ago. I ran into him in the bank. I was as
surprised to see him out here as you were to see Joan." She
thumped the pillows on her chaise longue. "He had changed a ·
lot. Pompous. The successful banker *with* paunch. I always
thought he'd go flabby. There's a little grey in his hair now, too.
Isabel, he looked years older."

"Then he didn't go back East after the divorce?" ·

"You didn't think his interest in Joan was paternal, I hope,"
Alice remarked. "He never got over her marrying Frank. I
think Thorne's the kind of person who gets what he wants, if it
takes a lifetime."

"Are you sure he had anything to do with Joan going to Reno?"

"Isabel, don't be naive. You know as well as I do—" She
shrugged, and reached for a cigarette. "They're engaged."

"Thorne and Joan?" I exclaimed.

Alice nodded.

"Exactly. He told me that afternoon. He's taken a house in
Bel-Air for the summer, and they plan to get married quietly at
Yuma or some place and move in for a while."

"Well, I suppose we might have guessed it," I said cautiously.
"I wonder how Frank feels about it?"

"I don't know." Alice seemed a little reluctant to reply; her
sympathies were obviously divided. "You know, Isabel, I never
understood just how things were between Joan and Frank. I
think he loved her as much as he could love any person. But
neither of them were ever anything but lilies of the field. They
didn't take well to being poor. That was the trouble, I'd say.
And if that's so, Joan seemed to me pretty cold-blooded about
leaving him the minute something better came along."

"Perhaps. On the other hand, Frank might have been to
blame."

"I know. That worries me," Alice admitted. I don't like to be
unfair to anybody. I wish I knew."

"I'm anxious now to see Joan Tuesday," I confessed. I'm
just as curious as you are, Alice, and for the same reason."

She looked at me suspiciously a moment.

"Do you think I'm a nosy old gossip, Isabel? Maybe it does
sound that way. Joan was my friend too, you know, even if she

did high-hat all of us every chance she got. She just was that way. I'd like to see her happy."

"So would I."

"Well, any way you look at it," she decided, "Thorne Emory had too many fingers in the pie. It certainly wasn't discreet, and I'm afraid he did more harm than good the way he's acted. Joan never should have sported that diamond bracelet the way she did—before the divorce. And Emory had no business staying in Reno while she was there. How could people help talking? Well," she added, "you'll see both of them, perhaps Tuesday, and find out just how things do stand."

"I think I will. And I'll bet right now that they're already married."

"Yes," she agreed. "That's the answer to the Rolls Royce and the finery. If not, they will be soon. Another drink, Isabel? How do you think the garden looks? I'm having a terrible time replacing the Japanese gardener. He was interned or something last week."

That was on Wednesday.

I went home, still curious, and eager for Tuesday to arrive. But as it happened, I did not have to wait that long.

On Thursday evening, about eight o'clock, Joan telephoned me.

I had dined alone at home that evening, and I had settled down in the den, with a big log fire going, because of the chill, when the phone rang. Feren, my maid, answered it and called me.

"A young lady," she announced from the hallway. "She won't give her name. She seems mighty anxious to talk to you, Miss Marsh."

"Very well," I said, and took up the receiver of the den extension.

Joan's voice, when I answered, was hardly recognizable.

"Oh, Isabel," she said, "I was so afraid I wouldn't be able to reach you!"

"Is anything the matter, Joan?"

"I'm worried. I'm being silly, I suppose. But I didn't know who else to turn to. Alice is the only other person I know out here, and I always felt she hated me. Can you do me a big favor?"

"I'll try, of course. What is it?" My first impulse had been to stay wisely aloof from Joan's problems, but the anxiety in her voice was too real.

"Can you come right over? I'm alone here, and frightened."

"Of course, if you want me to.  But I don't understand."

"Please hurry," she begged.  "It's the third house on your left as you turn off Sunset.  I'll have the driveway lights on."

I hung up and rose to find my hat.  All the time it took me to take the car out of the garage I kept telling myself I was simply asking for trouble by going over there.  The feeling actually oppressed me.  But no one could have listened to the helpless urgency in Joan's voice without answering her appeal.

## *Chapter* III

JOAN's house was a large stucco and timbered mansion in English style, buried in a wilderness of foliage.  A heavy screen of shrubbery blocked out the street completely, and ivy had climbed to the second story windows in thick masses. Even the entry was smothered under banana trees, and had the appearance of a separate thatched hut clapped onto the side of the house.

A light was burning in the midst of the banana fronds when I arrived, but it gave scanty illumination.  I drove my car through the gates and parked by the garage.  I had to walk from there along a narrow, winding path, with the branches of pepper trees brushing softly against my hat, and frightening me into dithers.  If I had owned the place, I would have started landscaping with an axe.

A white-faced maid in a black uniform opened the door for me.

"Miss Marsh?" she asked at once.  "You are expected.  Will you wait in the living-room?"

I nodded, and went into the dim room, where a low fire smouldered on a tremendous hearth.  The rest of the room was deeply shadowed.  I had only the impression of a ceiling supported by suspiciously artificial beams, and walls of a dull brown and faded oil paintings of punting on the Thames.

The room was empty when I entered, and chilly in spite of the fire.  The only light came from a large table lamp with a shade of opaque parchment.  French doors opened upon a terrace and the side lawn, I assumed, though it was too dark to see out clearly.

Joan came in almost running. It was a habit of hers to come hurrying in as if she were too eager to see you to dawdle. It made you feel welcome and very much as if you were a special event in Joan's life; until you got used to it. Then, if you are like me at all, you secretly hoped she'd trip over the rug the next time.

She certainly showed very little sign of being upset. I thought as I held out my hand to her, that she seemed to be particularly radiant, as if she had taken special pains with her toilet. More care, it seemed to me, than would have been necessary if she had merely wished me to sit and chat to keep her from being lonely. There was added color in her cheeks, however, besides her rouge, and her eyes were bright with some inner excitement.

"Isabel, what fun it is to see you again. We must sit down and tell each other everything that's happened to us for years. But how about a drink first?"

"I could do with a Scotch," I said, "after the way I rushed over. Is anything wrong, my dear?"

I thought she was rather evasive.

"No. Nothing, really. I'm expecting a visitor, and I—well, I didn't feel like having him here without—well, I wanted you here, that's all."

It wasn't like Joan suddenly to go conventional. I couldn't quite understand her.

"Someone I know?" I asked brightly. She ignored that.

"Thorne's out this evening. He may be home, though, and if he comes in, for heaven's sake keep him talking," she begged.

"Joan, don't tell me you brought me all the way out here just to keep Thorne from catching you with another man."

"Don't be ridiculous! I'm talking over business," she said quickly. "He wouldn't be interested. Or he might be too interested. I'm not being very clear, am I? But then, he probably won't be home until late."

"Joan, you *are* married to Thorne, then?"

"But of course! Didn't you know?"

"Alice told me you were engaged, but that's all I knew," I replied. "However, I'm not absolutely blind."

She flashed her wedding ring at me then, as if I hadn't already seen it and begun to wish I'd brought my sun glasses.

"Two weeks ago in Yuma," she said. "All very quiet, you know. Neither of us have many friends out here, and I didn't see any point in making a big affair of it, especially with the war and all."

"Much wiser," I said. "And, Joan, I do wish both of you every happiness. Thorne always did love you, I think."

"Ever since I was a kid. Think of the trouble I'd have saved if I hadn't been such an impulsive brat back East. Isabel, you've no idea—nobody has—what I went through with Frank. He was impossible!"

I felt suddenly awkward. I fervently hoped, that I would not have to listen to a recital of Frank Murdock's cruelties. I was in no mood for it, and I doubt if I would have been too sympathetic. But I was saved by the arrival of drinks. When I had settled back on a faded green sofa with mine, and the maid had gone, Joan brightened a little.

"But let's forget all that; it's over now, and I'm the happiest person alive—ecstatically happy."

"Is Elaine here with you?" I asked. Elaine was Joan's daughter. "How old is Elaine now?"

"Yes, she's here. She's thirteen, and she adores Thorne. That was the one thing that worried me."

I doubted that. Joan has a selfish streak in her and she seldom if ever allows herself to be worried about the likes and dislikes of others, once she has made up her own mind.

"How does she like California?" I inquired, determined to keep the conversation to safe topics.

"She loves it. But she doesn't know many people. I want to put her in school as soon as I can."

We discussed schools for a while, I remember; and gradually my uneasiness began to abate. I was startled when the door bell rang shrilly. Joan jumped up hurriedly.

"Please stay here, Isabel, until I come back," she begged. "I won't be gone long. I'll send Sarah in with another Scotch. I hate to leave you, but be a lamb and help me."

She took my acquiescence for granted, and hurried from the room. She must have reached the front door before Sarah, because I heard it open, and the murmur of her voice, and a man's. If I had stood up and moved half a dozen steps to the right I could have seen who it was. I was terribly tempted to do it, too, but some fleeting surge of ancestral honor, I suppose, prevented me. I listened to her low, hurried voice, and the man's. Then I heard them go up the stairs together.

I was burning with curiosity, and I determined not to leave the house before I had had some sort of explanation from Joan.

But for a while nothing happened. I looked at an old copy of *Vogue* that lay on the table, and then a *National Geographic,* until recollections of waiting in a dentist's office became too vivid, and I had to toss them aside.

I began wandering around the room then, looking at the pictures, but they lacked emotional wallop. They were too grimy even to be distinct.

So finally I drifted to the French doors and glanced out.

It was a bright night, with a full moon just topping the eucalyptus trees by the street. A silvery light poured down on the lawn, and the high hedge at the end of it. To my right, toward the back of the house, the grounds dropped down sharply to a narrow ravine where, I learned later, there were paths and rustic benches beside a little brook, usually dried up. Here, again, the shrubbery was so thick that it made my flesh crawl at the mere thought of the bugs it sheltered.

It was so bright outside that I could have counted the blades of grass, if I had been closer to them. But among these bushes, smooth-leafed avocados, mock-oranges, and clumps of oleander, it was black as pitch. I must have been looking at them for a minute or more before I realized that there was a shadow there that should not have been there.

It was indistinct, but in the still night, with no air stirring, it moved. It had shape, too, and it was a human shape.

I don't think I was alarmed at first. I was merely curious. But there was something so silent, so furtive about the movements of the shadow that it frightened me.

The room I was in was almost dark, and the shadows by the window must have hidden me. If there was a man hiding out there in the garden, I did not think he would see me. But I drew back into the room hastily, and found I was shaking, and my arms were covered with goose pimples.

There was no use trying to tell myself not to be silly; that it was probably the chauffeur out for a late smoke. The garage was empty; I'd seen that when I parked my own car.

Impulsively, I shut off the lamp, and crossed to a window that opened upon the back. A path skirted the edge of the ravine there, and the shadow was moving slowly along it, vague and blurred against the screen of shrubbery. I could see now that it was a man, but there was no chance of recognizing him. He wore a hat pulled down over his face.

. For a moment I felt panicky. My knees were shaking so badly that I could not move. Only that kept me from rushing out into the hall, screaming. Instead, when I could I groped my way toward the hall door.

I heard someone coming down the steps, then, and for some reason my fright vanished. I started to call out, but checked myself abruptly. I was being absurd, I knew. Joan would come in in a moment, and turn on the light, and I would tell her I was only looking at the moonlight, and ask her if a butler or valet happened to be outside . . .

The footsteps paused, and I heard a man's voice, loud and distinct, say suddenly, "Good Lord! Don't!"

Then there was a thunderous crash that took my breath away.

How I reached the doorway I don't know. I stood there a moment, too dazed to comprehend anything. Then, gradually, things began to fall into focus. I saw a dim light burning over the steps, a pale amber bulb in a lantern-shaped shade. Joan and Thorne Emory were running down the steps, and below them, sprawled in a heap at the foot of the stairs, was the body of a man.

He gave a convulsive movement, coughed, and lay still.

Then, I think, I did scream. I clung to the doorway for support, while blood spread over the man's shirt front, and his eyes, glassy and unseeing, stared at me.

I had only seen him once in ten years, and that had been only a glimpse across a busy street. But I had not an instant's doubt as to who he was. And like some hysterical Lady Macbeth, I heard Joan's shrill voice, raised almost to a shout.

"Thorne! Oh, my God, it's Frank! Dead! Here in my house!"

## Chapter IV

THORNE paid no attention to her. I don't suppose he even saw me standing in the living-room doorway, against the heavy darkness. He paused for a moment beside the body, bending over it; and his face, hardly visible in the shadows thrown by the one amber lamp, was inscrutable.

He looked up at a door opposite the foot of the stairs. Joan was clinging to the banister, halfway down the steps, and her breath was coming in heavy gasps that were almost sobs. I wanted to run to her, but that huddled body lying between us was a barrier that my shattered nerves could not pass.

Thorne had vanished into the room opposite the steps. The lights sprang on in there, and, as if they were a magnet drawing me, I hurried in after him.

It was a small room panelled in pickled pine, and lined with book cases. The far wall seemed to be composed entirely of windows. At first I was surprised not to see Thorne anywhere; then I realized that there was a door, open to the grounds.

"Thorne!" I cried, and reached out as if I could catch him and drag him back into the room, away from the danger lurking out there in the dark.

His heavy figure suddenly filled the doorway as he returned.

"Isabel Marsh!" he exclaimed, surprised, when he saw me. "I didn't know you were here. How did you get here?"

"Joan called me and asked me. Thorne, what happened? I saw a man outside there a minute ago!"

"You did?" He stood uncertainly in the middle of the room, his broad face flushed, and his greying hair damp and sleek on his perfectly round head. "He was standing in the doorway there when I came down," he said heavily.

"Did you recognize him?"

"No." He shook his head. "It was too dark. I'd just come from a bright room upstairs. I only saw his figure. He must have fired the shot. There's nowhere else it could have come from, except from the living-room."

"Oh, no! I was there!" I exclaimed.

"That door was open to the yard," he said, inclining his head toward it.

Joan was calling wildly to him from the stairway.

"Thorne! Thorne! Where are you? Don't leave me alone here!" she cried, and there was a note of hysteria in her voice. We rushed out to the hall together. She had staggered down the rest of the steps, drawing away from the body with a convulsive shudder. When she saw us she threw herself into Thorne's arms and began to weep. Awkardly he began patting her shoulder.

"There, there, Joany! Don't do that! It's all right. It's all right. Isabel, ring for the maid, will you?"

But there was no need to do that. Two frightened women, their figures like thin ghosts, were peering in from the dining room, afraid to come a step closer.

"Bring Mrs. Emory some ammonia!" Thorne called to them. "Upstairs in the bathroom medicine closet. Doris, you fix her a dose and bring it here right away."

The women melted away into the obscurity.

"Hadn't you better call a doctor?" I demanded. "Thorne, Frank's badly hurt."

He hesitated for a moment before he answered, gently pressing Joan's head against his shoulder. His voice was perfectly calm when he spoke, and I felt a little shock, and perhaps the vaguest touch of envy, at his self-control.

"He's dead, Isabel," he said quietly. "Too late for a doctor. We'd better call the police."

"The man outside will get away!" I wailed. "Oh, Thorne, what can we do?"

"I'm not going to look for him," he said flatly. "He's just shot one man. I don't think he'd hesitate to shoot me. Let the police trace him, if they can."

He began to lead Joan, still shaking with sobs, into the living-room.

"If you don't mind, Isabel," he called over his shoulder, "I wish you'd phone the police. I'm afraid to leave Joan."

"Of course! Where's the phone?"

"There's one in the library. But perhaps you'd rather use the one upstairs," he suggested.

"And—and climb over that—the body? Oh, Thorne, I *couldn't!*"

"There are back steps going up from the kitchen. Just go through the dining-room."

He switched on the living-room lights. Their glow threw a patch of light into the dining-room, illuminating faintly a door beyond leading to the kitchen. I hurried through, a little breathlessly, and found the back steps. The upper hall was well lighted, and almost at once I saw the sitting-room, which was directly over the library below. The phone was on a table near the door.

I called Captain Branson. He had been in charge of the Dodge murder, and I knew him well.

I found him finally at his own home, and told him somewhat confusedly what had happened.

"It's terrible, Al," I said. "Joan is hysterical and Thorne as black as a thundercloud. Please get out here as fast as you can, before we all go completely haywire."

"Coming at once," he said briskly. "Listen, Isabel, have everybody stay away from the body, and keep those bright eyes of yours open. Have you any idea who did it?"

"No. None at all, yet. Somebody was hiding out in the grounds, and probably came in through the library door. That's just opposite the steps. But you'll see for yourself when you get here. And please hurry."

"You bet I will."

He hung up, then, and I sat for a moment beside the phone, too cowardly, I confess, to go back downstairs and pass that horrible lifeless thing lying by the steps. Frank Murdock, as I had known him, had been too handsome for his own good. The years had not changed that, except, perhaps, to add character to a face once youthful and a trifle weak. But now what lay at the foot of the steps was no longer Frank Murdock. It was a discarded shell of corruption and horror, like a sleeping monster that had slipped in from another world.

I thought of the ammonia in the bathroom closet, and went to look for it. I was completely unfamiliar with the house, but after all, bathrooms are not difficult to find, and I reached Joan's just as a girl, dressed in dark blue, was coming out of it. She was pretty, in a dark half-Spanish way, though her face was broad and a little hard.

She murmured an apology as she stood aside, regarding me with eyes suspiciously reddened.

"Are you Doris?" I asked her. She nodded.

"I'm Miss Elaine's governess," she explained. "I've just taken Mrs. Emory her ammonia. Can I fix a dose for you?"

"Thanks, I can get it for myself. I feel a little shaken too."

"A little!" she exclaimed, and her lips began to quiver. "It's too horrible! That poor man! It was an evil day for him when he met Mrs. Emory!"

Her eyes were blazing with a deadly anger. I looked at her in astonishment.

"Really, Doris—what *is* your name?"

She answered mechanically, her hands clenched at her sides.

"Ayers," she said without embellishment.

"Really, Miss Ayers, don't you think you're being a bit—?" I shrugged then and did not finish what I had started to say. It was no business of mine to rebuke Joan's employees for disloyalty. Miss Ayers fixed her eyes on me, and the anger in them had not abated.

"That man was murdered by Mrs. Emory," she said stonily, "just as certainly as if her hand held the gun."

"Miss Ayers, please! You're forgetting yourself!"

"No. I'm not. I'm not accusing her of anything but hounding him to death. He loved her once. I know. And she drove him to his death with her love of money and fine things. And Elaine! How is that child ever going to live down the shame of having her own father shot dead in the usurper's house?"

She pushed past me then, and went down the hall. Her dark head was thrown back, and she walked like one half dazed.

When I mixed the ammonia for myself after that, I made it a double dose. I needed it badly.

## Chapter V

JOAN was crying without control when I returned to the living-room. She was lying on a faded green velour couch, and Thorne was sitting on an ottoman beside her, trying ineffectually to quiet her. He glanced up as I came in.

"Isabel, see if you can do anything with her," he begged. "The shock's been too much for her."

"I don't wonder," I said. But for some reason I did not feel the sympathy for her I should have. Perhaps Doris Ayers' impassioned words upstairs had affected me more than I realized. "I've heard that slapping a person's face sometimes snaps them out," I suggested helpfully.

He looked slightly shocked.

"Slap her? Oh, I can't do that! I think she ought to go upstairs to her room and lie down. Doris can sit with her, while I talk to the police."

"Doris. Or the maid," I added.

"The maid," he agreed, with an odd expression. "Yes. Can you help me get her upstairs, do you think?"

By the time we had got her upstairs and comfortably settled in bed, her sobs had ceased. The first thing she asked for was a damp cloth and her compact, and I went downstairs again, less alarmed about her condition.

And then the police were there, dozens of them, with cameras and fingerprint outfits. Al Branson was with them, and he seemed to me like a Gibraltar of strength and comfort. It was all I could do to keep from rushing into his arms, but in front of all those members of the Homicide Squad that simply wouldn't have done.

I remember saying over and over, "Oh, Al! I shouldn't have come here tonight. I shouldn't!"

"Now, now, easy, there!" he warned me. "Run along into the living-room and wait there, Isabel. I'll be in, in a moment."

I could hear Thorne clearing his throat and beginning to explain, as I went in and sat down.

"I understand you're from the Sheriff's office?"

Al admitted he was.

"Well, I'm Thorne Emory. You probably know who I am."

"I can't say I do, Mr. Emory," Al remarked courteously.

"Anyone will tell you. I'm President of the Union National Bank, and director of—never mind that now. The point is I want as little trouble here as possible. This—accident has been quite a shock to my wife. I'm interested in sparing her as much as possible."

Al simply grunted.

"You understand, don't you?" asked Thorne.

"Perfectly," said Al suavely. I could imagine the very unsympathetic look in his usually friendly eyes. Al had had altogether too much of that attitude of "You don't know who I am" interfering with his work in the past. Thorne had made the worst possible impression in the beginning. But I suppose, being Thorne Emory, he couldn't have been expected to do otherwise. "Shall we join Miss Marsh in the living-room? You can tell me what happened then."

They came in, Al steering him expertly, without seeming to do so.

"Just sit down here, Mr.—er, Emory, is it? That's it. Now let's get the thing straight from the beginning. I understand you are living here with your wife. Now who is the dead man? Miss Marsh did not tell me over the phone."

"He is Frank Murdock, my wife's former husband," said Thorne, taking the most comfortable chair, and settling himself in it as if he were presiding at a directors' meeting. Al's eyebrows rose slightly, but he made no comment. "He had called this evening—well, perhaps I'd better explain," Thorne added uncomfortably.

"Yes?"

"My wife was divorced from him several months ago. She and I have been married about two weeks. About a week ago I received a communication from the legal firm of Post, Hurley and Stebbins that Mr. Murdock was—er—instituting alienation proceedings." He paused and cleared his throat, glancing at me apologetically. Obviously he was very uncomfortable indeed.

"The man had no grounds—absolutely none!" he exclaimed vehemently. "And yet he had the audacity to bring suit against me for one half million dollars!"

My eyes must have been popping out of my head, for Al looked at me curiously, and shook his head slightly, warning me not to interrupt. But I was too surprised to speak just then.

"I would have contested the case to the last ditch," Thorne declared. "He hadn't a leg to stand on. As a matter of fact, I believe I could have had the whole thing thrown out of court. But in any case, the publicity would have been most embarrassing.

"Tonight I went to consult my own legal adviser. . . ."

"Who is he, may I ask?"

"Arthur Sherman."

"Oh, yes. I know him," said Al. "At what time was this, exactly?"

"I left here about seven-thirty, as a matter of fact," said Thorne. He sat up very straight in his chair, the tips of the fingers of both hands pressed together. "I did not have an appointment, but I wanted to see him, and I took a chance of finding him at home."

"Did you?"

"No. No, I didn't. He was out, and I left a message, and returned here at once."

"I gather you didn't take the precaution of telephoning him first."

"Well, yes, I did. I called his butler, who assured me he would probably be in all evening. I left word I would be there before eight. But for some reason he was detained at his office, at least so the butler told me when I arrived."

"I see. You got back here at what time?"

"Approximately eight-thirty."

"And when did Mr. Murdock arrive?"

Thorne stirred uncomfortably in his chair.

"I couldn't say. You see, my wife was a little unwise. She tried to help, I feel convinced. But she acted very foolishly."

"In what way, Mr. Emory?"

"She found out from someone—I don't know who—where Mr. Murdock was living, and she telephoned him. I appreciate her motives. She had some hope, I believe, of inducing Mr. Murdock to drop the suit, or at least to accept settlement. Even though the suit wouldn't have held up in court for a moment, she naturally dreaded the publicity. You understand?"

"Oh, quite. Go on, please."

"She knew I would be out this evening, and I feel sure she expected me to be at Mr. Sherman's until quite late. She made an appointment with Mr. Murdock to meet her here this evening at eight. I don't quite know what she intended saying to him. She certainly could not have expected to appeal to his better nature. He had none. The very fact of his bringing suit proves that, I think. But in any case, she hoped to persuade him somehow. Naturally I knew nothing of this, or I would have forbidden it absolutely. It was *most* indiscreet."

He took a cigarette absently from a gold case without offering us one, and lighted it. I saw that his hands were unsteady.

"I came back about eight-fifteen, as I told you," he went on, after a moment or two. "I suppose I ought to explain that it is rather awkward to reach the front door from the driveway that leads to the garage. It's very overgrown, and at night branches are always knocking against one's head. If the house were mine, I'd cut down several of the pepper trees—but, of course, I'm only renting.

"My wife and I make a habit of coming in through the kitchen, and either coming in here through the dining-room, or going directly upstairs by the servants' stairs. That's what I did this evening. I found her in the upstairs sitting-room with Mr. Murdock."

"What happened?" Al asked, when the silence seemed to drag out unduly.

"There was no scene at all," Thorne said, with satisfaction. "I was surprised, naturally. But nothing really happened. Murdock was much more embarrassed than I was. I think he made some remark, but I don't remember what it was. I told him to leave the house at once, and not to return. I asked my wife to go to

her room, until I had seen him to the door, and she went immediately.

"I'm trying to be very accurate now," he explained, "because
I realize how important the next minute is. My wife was in her
room. Mr. Murdock had already started down the steps when I
started down after him.

"Then I heard him speak. I thought at first he was talking to
me, but he was looking toward the library door, which is directly
opposite the foot of the steps out there."

"Do you remember what he said?"

"Not the exact words. Something like, 'Don't shoot me!' "

"He said, 'Good Lord! Don't!' " I interrupted. "I heard him
distinctly."

"I'll hear what you have to say later, Isabel," Al said, nodding
to me. "But thanks, anyway."

"Not at all," I remarked, subsiding.

"Go on, Mr. Emory, please."

"Well, it was rather confusing then. Someone fired a shot,
and Murdock plunged down the steps. My wife ran out of her
room and came down the stairs after me."

"You didn't see anyone fire the shot, then?"

"No. I didn't see anyone. Miss Marsh was standing in the living-room doorway, but it was so dark I didn't even notice her
at first."

"Have you any idea where the shot came from?"

Thorne paused to think.

"I couldn't be certain; it was so sudden, so completely unexpected. But I'm sure the only place it could have come from was
the library. Miss Marsh was in the living-room, so it couldn't have
come from there. The dining-room is opposite it, as you may have
noticed, but I hardly think it came from there. The maid and
Mrs. Emory's daughter's governess were in the kitchen and anyone coming in that way would have had to pass them. I'm sure
they'd have stopped any stranger, or called out. No, the library is
the obvious place, especially since Miss Marsh saw someone lurking in the grounds out that way.

"She called my attention to that, and I went into the library to
investigate. I found a door in there, which leads out to the grounds,
standing open."

"I see. Is that door usually closed?"

"I couldn't say. We use it now and then, but it's always locked before we retire. It *could* have been left open, I imagine, this early in the evening."

"Did you go outside to investigate?"

"Just for a moment. I didn't see anyone, so I returned."

"Thanks. I believe that's all for the time being, except one thing. Have you any idea who might have made an attack on Mr. Murdock?"

"I cannot imagine. I knew him very slightly in the past few years, and I couldn't possibly tell you anything about his private life."

"Thanks again."

"If that's all you wish to know now, I'd appreciate it if you'd let me go up to see how my wife is getting along. The shock was pretty severe and she's lying down."

"Go ahead, Mr. Emory. I'd like to talk to her, too, later."

"That will be quite impossible tonight," Thorne declared firmly. "She's in no condition to be troubled."

I thought to myself that Joan, whatever else she was, certainly was no frail, swooning woman. True, the shock undoubtedly had upset her, as it had me, but I was willing to wager that within half an hour she'd be as capable of answering questions as Thorne was.

## Chapter VI

"**D**o you think Thorne went upstairs for a reason?" I asked Al, the minute he'd gone.

"What do you mean, Isabel?"

"Couldn't he have been planning to talk to Joan alone? I wouldn't put it past him to—what do you call it?—suppress evidence, or whatever it is. Anything to avoid publicity. He's good at avoiding scandal. He's just steered Joan through the juiciest divorce case I ever heard of, and not a line of it leaked into the papers. That's odd, too, because with all his bluster, Thorne is a millionaire at least, and really important."

"You don't like him, do you?" Al asked, studying me closely, smiling a little.

"Frankly, no. He somehow reminds me a little of an overgrown garden slug. He's a stuffed shirt."

"A slug in a stuffed shirt. Slightly balled up metaphor, but picturesque, Isabel. What have you to add to what he said?"

"Nothing, Al, except that I want to get home as soon as I can, and get out of this creepy house. I wish I'd never come in the first place."

"Why did you come?"

"Well, Joan begged me so."

"It isn't like you to get mixed up in things like this. Not the murder. I mean the divorce business, the alienation suit."

"I swear I didn't know a thing about that until Thorne told you just now. If I had, I wouldn't have come. Joan knew it, too. I'm sure that's why she didn't tell me. She was evasive all evening.

"Did she tell you Murdock was coming?"

"Of course not! She just mentioned that a guest was coming and she wanted me in the house as a sort of chaperone. And she didn't even tell me that until after I got here."

"I wonder if she was putting one over on her husband?"

"That's what I thought, too. I guess I still do, a little. She acted odd all evening."

"Well—" He stood up. "You wait here a minute, while I take another look around out there. Then I'll drop you at your home."

They had taken Frank's body away, so I went as far as the living-room door with him, and watched. There wasn't much for the fingerprint experts to do, except to try the knob of the library door for marks, but the photographers were still taking flash shots of the steps and the hall and the den.

Al drew the police doctor aside.

"Anything about the body you can tell me?" he asked.

The doctor spread his hands, and stuck out his lower lip.

"Nothing at all you didn't see for yourself, Captain. He died pretty quickly. Shot through the heart. Don't know the calibre yet, but not heavy."

"Was the shot fired from directly in front of him, or from the side?"

"Directly in front."

"And that looks like it came from the library."

"Yes," said the doctor cautiously. "Unless he saw someone in the hall and turned to look to one side or the other. But I'd say it's logical to assume that the person who shot him stood about in the library door."

"From what distance, would you estimate?"

"Oh, I can't say to the inch. The library door would be about right, though. Anything else? If not, I think I'll run along, and give you a report when I've probed for the bullet, and made a closer examination."

"O. K. Good night." Al turned to one of the detectives, a man named Green whom I remembered quite well from the Dodge case. He nodded to me pleasantly. "Find anything, Green?"

"Nothing much, Captain. Plenty of fingerprints on the door knob. It will be a job to sort 'em out. That's about all. The stiff had a wallet on him with a couple of visiting cards, twelve dollars in bills, and a couple of three cent stamps. Picture of a little girl, cut out of a snapshot, I'd say, tucked in a corner. Then he had some change, and a couple of letters addressed to him."

"What's the address?"

"Somewhere near Santa Monica boulevard and La Brea," said Green. "I know the place. It's an auto court. Cheap little one and two-room apartments."

"O.K. Who were the letters from?"

"One was from a woman, in El Paso. Wanted to know when her Musty would be back to see Texas. Her husband is now stationed at some camp in the East, and she's awful lonely. I quoted that last."

"I thought you did, Green. Your grammar may not always be impeccable, but I detected the quotation. The other letter?"

"A reminder that he had promised to take care of a grocery bill in Austin, and hadn't yet done so. Very polite, firm, and a little as if they knew it was hopeless but tried anyhow."

"Good. Nothing else?"

"No. Nothing on him."

"Did you look around outside? Miss Marsh here, you know, thought she saw a man out there before the shot was fired."

"I heard," said Green. "Sure. I looked. Ryan's out there now with a flashlight. Shall I call him?"

"No. Wait till he comes in. Find out what servants there are."

"Four. A couple; she's the cook, and he's butler and doubles as chauffeur. This is their night out, and they haven't come in yet. Then there's Sarah Bentley; she's the upstairs maid. And a tony governess named Ayers—and that's her all over, Captain."

"Did you find out anything from them?"

"Ayers got high hat. You'd think she owned the joint. Didn't know anything. The maid, same story. Said she and Ayers were having a cup of tea in the kitchen. They saw Emory come in about five minutes before the shot. He used the back door because it's near the garage. Then he went right up the back steps. They were together there when they heard the shot, and they were scared pink. But Ayers raises her eyebrows and decides to take a look. So they went to the dining-room and looked. By that time the excitement was all over."

"I see. Did either of them see anybody hanging around outside?"

"No. They'd yelled their heads off, both of them, if they had, if you ask me."

"All right, Green. I'll tackle Ayers myself later, but I don't suppose she'll help much."

Ryan came in from the garden just then, scraping mud off his boots at the door. I remembered him, too. Once I had almost got him into trouble by telling Al that he had been asleep when he should have been on guard at an empty house. That he had forgiven me I considered very flattering.

He stared at me open-mouthed when he came in.

"Holy smoke, Miss Marsh, are you mixed up in this one too?" he demanded.

"Only as a spectator, Ryan," I assured him.

"Yeah. I know." He wagged his head wisely.

"Really. All I want to do is go home and forget all about it."

He grinned at me, with a knowing leer "I'll bet," he said, unconvinced.

"Did you find anything, Ryan?" Al interrupted our little conversation.

"No man out there. Here's the gun." He held out something that was identified for me later as a Colt .25. At the time it merely looked small but wicked. But then, I have never trusted firearms, having always believed they have a sort of will of their own, like robots.

Al took it carefully, by the pencil which Ryan had thrust through the trigger guard. It looked frosted, covered as it was with dew.

"Where was it?" Al asked.

Ryan pointed out the door vaguely.

"There's a path out there that zigzags down to a gully and a brook. I found it lying beside the path just after the first bend."

Al called the fingerprint man and handed it to him.

"I wonder how he happened to drop it," he said, puzzled. "He must have been pretty rattled."

"Well, why wouldn't he be?" I demanded. "I would, I know. If I dropped the darn thing in that darkness out there I certainly wouldn't wait to look for it."

"Not if you knew your fingerprints were on it, or it could be traced?"

I hadn't thought of that. But when Al pointed it out, the objection didn't seem to be insurmountable.

"You told me yourself," I said, "that practically every murderer you came across was almost rabid on the subject of fingerprints these days. If somebody came here tonight to kill Frank Murdock, he probably wore gloves."

"He'd only do that, Isabel, if he intended to toss the gun away in the bushes. And why, for the love of mike, would he do that?"

"That's easy," I said at once. I hadn't read lots of detective stories for nothing. "It was somebody else's gun. He'd want it found to point suspicion to somebody else."

"Your brother once said you had a lurid mind," Al said sadly. "I'm afraid I agree with him. We'll take it for granted the murderer was rattled and had no intention of dropping the gun. Do you agree?"

I shrugged.

"Really, Al, I don't know. I won't agree with you. I wish I'd never come here, and I want to go home. I wish you'd just let me go. My car's out there."

"No. Wait," he said. "I may need you. Anything else, Ryan?"

"No, sir That's a gravel path down there, and it doesn't show footprints. Not ones you could measure, anyway. If anyone ran along that path, he didn't leave any signs. He could have got out easy, too. The path winds down past the badminton court, and from there to the street. It's just a few yards, and all shaded. And in two minutes he'd be on Sunset Boulevard."

Al shook his head.

"Well, I guess that's about all, Ryan. I'll carry on here awhile. Find out if there were any prints on that gun, will you? And trace it for me."

"O.K., Captain." He touched his forehead in an informal salute and moved away. Al drew me into the library.

"I know how you feel about all this, Isabel," he began apologetically "You want to go home. But I need your help."

"No, Al. Please. I've learned my lesson, and I cry quits. Please."

"It's not a great deal, Isabel."

I sighed, and capitulated.

"What is it, then? But don't go getting any ideas, Al Branson, that your big blue eyes influence me. My judgment tells me to say good night firmly at this point, and drive away from here."

"I'm afraid your friend Emory is going to be difficult about seeing his wife. And I want a talk with her."

"I can't arrange it for you," I assured him hastily, "if that's what you're driving at."

"No. I wondered if you couldn't talk to her yourself."

"Al, would that be quite—well, honorable? She's my friend, you know."

He patted my shoulder consolingly.

"If *she's* honorable, she'll want to see justice done," he pointed out. "If she isn't, you still are. You knew Frank Murdock, too. Someone shot him down, Isabel."

I pondered that for a while.

"All right," I agreed at last. "What do I ask her?"

## *Chapter* VII

A SINGLE light burned under a mauve silk shade in Joan's room. It was a large room at the front of the house, with windows almost blocked with ivy, facing the street and the gardens at the side. Everywhere a decorator had hung taffeta, in shades of violet, lilac, and purple. There were accents of turquoise here and there. The whole effect was lush, feminine, and theatrical. Somehow it did not clash with Joan's temperament at all. It might have been designed especially as a setting for the person she considered herself to be; and which she was, with important modifications.

She was sitting up in bed, between sheets of pale heliotrope, and wearing a turquoise negligee. She had a stiff Scotch in her hand when I went in, which somewhat shattered the illusion of fragility she otherwise presented. Other than two bright pink spots in her cheeks, she was quite calm again, and showed no sign of shock. Her weeping had ceased long ago.

"Oh, Isabel!" she exclaimed, when she saw me. "Isn't all this mess plain hell?"

"It's not exactly a picnic," I retorted. "How are you feeling?"

"Like a rag. There: sit down on the bed and tell me what happened."

"The police have been examining everything," I said, sinking up to my hips in the soft mattress. "They found the gun out there in the yard, but that's about all."

"I wish they'd go away and leave us alone! Wouldn't you know Frank would be inconsiderate right up to the bitter end, and die here, of all places?"

"I don't suppose he chose to die," I said drily. "And I believe you were the one who asked him to come here."

"Don't be catty, Isabel," Joan pleaded, putting an exquisitely manicured hand on my arm. "I didn't mean that. I'm just jittery. It *was* a mistake to ask him here. I should have known better."

"Listen, Joan," I said impulsively, "I don't know anything about you and Frank and your troubles. I've been out of touch with you both for so many years, you're almost like strangers to me. But, after all, Frank was married to you for a long time. Don't you think you're being a little too cold-blooded about this? After all, you loved him once."

"Don't be silly! He was impossible! I'm not going to be a hypocrite and pretend to be sorry—not for a minute." She finished her drink, and set the glass down on her bed table. "If he'd lived, he'd have dragged us through as rotten and smelly a trial as you could ask for. No matter who won it, Thorne's reputation wouldn't have been worth a cent afterwards. Why should I pretend to feel anything but relief? I hated him with every inch of my soul."

"Well, if you're going to measure your soul in inches—!" I got up, and started to walk around the room. I hated what I was doing; and I began to like Joan less and less. "You're not helping Thorne any, you know. Don't go around telling the police how much you hated Frank, or they'll make trouble."

"I'm not going to even talk to them," she said, with decision. "Thorne will fix that. They won't know how I feel, unless you tell them."

"Joan, listen to me." I stopped beside the bed and looked down at her. In that moment I felt like spanking her. "I'm not in a position to tell you what to do. But I know a little about the police, after all. And my advice to you is to ask Captain Branson to come up here right now, and tell him everything you can that would help him. And try to show a little respect, if you can't pretend grief, for poor Frank."

She drew her teeth slowly over her lower lip.

"Thanks for the advice. But you admit I wouldn't help Thorne, if I said anything. And I couldn't hide, for a minute, how I felt about that man. No, Isabel, I stay in bed, under a doctor's care, until this is all straightened out. Thorne and Mr. Sherman can fix that up."

I was becoming a little exasperated.

"Joan" I said, "do you know anything about Frank's death at all?"

"No."

"Have you any idea who might have been outside there in the grounds?"

"If you mean, do I know anybody who might have shot Frank, I'd say, instantly, yes, anybody who knew him."

I controlled my temper as well as I could.

"I never heard that Frank was that bad," I remarked. "What was the matter with him?"

"Oh, everything!" She flicked her fingers in the air, as if to dismiss him completely. "He was a lazy loafer, and a bum, and he couldn't keep his eye off every pretty woman he saw. He—"

"Let's be specific. What women? Can you name any?"

"I think I could name plenty, if I had to," she said spitefully. "You don't believe me, do you, Isabel? Well, I won't satisfy you. I won't drag anybody else into this. But if you're looking for one of Frank's fair victims, I don't think you'd have to look far."

"Just what do you mean by that?"

"Oh, nothing. Hand me that bell, will you, dear? I want to ring for Doris, and see if Elaine's all right."

I handed her a small bronze bell that stood on the bed table. I was a little dazed, and I stood at the window, staring out at a street lamp, while she rang. I saw clearly what she meant, then. And the worst of it was that Miss Ayers herself had taken an attitude that only seemed to confirm it.

I waited as patiently as I could while Miss Ayers came in, and assured Joan that Elaine was asleep.

"She doesn't know anything's happened yet," said Miss Ayers, very formally. "I explained the shot to her as an electric light bulb dropping. I don't believe she doubted it."

"Thank you, Doris. See that she sleeps well."

"Yes, Mrs. Emory." Miss Ayers nodded, and left. Joan was smiling to herself when I turned away from the window.

"When did they meet?" I asked bluntly.

"In Reno. Frank turned up there after we'd served him the papers. He didn't contest the divorce, you know. But I found out afterwards he'd been meeting Elaine on the street every day—taking her for walks, or rides, buying her little presents; trying, of course, to turn her against me."

"Isn't it just possible, Joan, that he loved his daughter?"

"Pshaw!" she said scornfully. "Frank never loved anyone in his life but himself!"

"How do you know about Doris Ayers and Frank?"

"I have eyes, haven't I? Do you know the girl actually had the impertinence to try to talk me out of the divorce? That's how I knew she'd been talking to Frank. Frank was using *her* to get around me!"

"I notice, though, that you've kept her here."

She avoided my eyes, and did not reply for a moment.

"Would she have been a witness for you if the alienation suit had come up?" I demanded. Joan answered in so low a voice I scarcely heard her.

"No, Isabel. But she might have been Frank's witness."

"I see."

"Don't you realize how damaging she might have been?" Joan exclaimed, with sudden vehemence. "Frank had made love to her. She was wrapped around his finger. She'd have said anything on the witness stand he wanted her to; perjured herself black and blue for him. Silly susceptible fool!"

I sighed and sat down again, on a chair this time; and that too was too softly cushioned, so I felt as if I were stuck on top of a big roasted marshmallow.

"Then, even as long ago as that, you knew Frank was going to bring suit," I said.

"He threatened it. I didn't believe he would, but Doris told me he might. So I took Thorne's advice and kept her close to me, so she'd be under our eyes all the time."

"Joan, you don't think she's been seeing him here, do you?" I asked, the idea suddenly striking me.

"I hadn't thought of it. I don't know. Perhaps."

"Well, the police will certainly find out."

She shrugged, as if that were unimportant now.

"The police will probably nose into everything we do," she declared bitterly. "But I'm not worried. Don't forget Frank had a life of his own that I didn't share at all. There's plenty there for them to chew on. I don't mind telling you, Isabel, that if Frank's suit had ever come into court, we'd have sprung enough evidence to blast him completely. Suppose Thorne and I had seen a lot of each other. Frank's hands weren't clean. Not so you could notice it! Oh, we knew things. Women—married women. I know of one man right now who could bring suit against Frank if he wanted to. And I'm not going to tell you who, either, so don't ask me. That's over now. And I daresay there were others."

"Joan, there's one thing I don't understand. If you felt this way about Frank, why did you ask him to come here tonight? What in the world did you expect to gain by it?"

She looked at me steadily for a long moment.

"I don't expect you to understand," she replied finally. "I did have some influence over Frank. I didn't love him a bit. But in spite of that—maybe because of that—I could make him do anything I wanted. I could talk to him in a way Thorne or the lawyers never could. I was going to do three things, if Thorne hadn't interrupted. One of the three would have worked. First I was going to beg him to think of Elaine and her future. I didn't expect to get far with that, and I didn't. He accused me pretty flatly of not having thought of it myself, and told me that—well, anyway, that didn't move him.

"Then I offered him a hundred thousand dollars. He only laughed at that. He was so blasted sure of himself. That was when Thorne came in. If he hadn't, I still think I could have managed Frank. Because, Isabel, I was going to quote chapter and verse to him, and show him pretty plainly that I knew about a certain affair. Oh, I was going to put the fear of the Lord in him! I could have, too. But I didn't have time."

She was sitting up very straight in her bed now, looking at the far wall with eyes that flashed hatred. I don't think she even heard me get up, or say good night. She was still sitting that way, an odd little smile on her lips, when I went out.

I walked quickly to the steps.

"This time," I told myself firmly, "I *am* going home. And I'm through being the good Samaritan."

But I was completely wrong on both points.

## *Chapter* VIII

I T WAS the first time I had descended the front steps, and I confess I felt a little odd as I went down, even though I knew perfectly well that Frank's body had been taken away long ago in one of those horrible brown canvas carriers that seem to rob death of all its dignity.

The stairs were narrow and steep. They descended sharply to a small landing, over which the iron lantern hung, optimistically pouring out its faint amber light. There was a high window in the wall, useless as a means of vision but giving, I suppose, a little light in the daytime. Then the steps turned and dropped away to the lower hall.

I paused for a moment just at the head of that second flight. The library door was in front of me, but it was in darkness again, and I wondered how well I could have seen a figure standing there. I decided he would have been visible but not easily recognized if he had been directly in the doorway. If he had stood back a few feet I don't think I could have seen him at all. The room beyond was too dark.

On my right was the wide archway leading to the dining-room; on the left, the living-room where I had been. The front door was beside, and to the left of the stairs. For an instant I wondered whether anyone might have stood there and fired the shot. I could see it easily as I leaned over the banister, and I realized that I would be an easy target to anyone there as I did so. But the door was of heavy wood, with a massive lock, and looked impregnable, except for the small peephole in the upper panel.

I shook my head and continued down.

There were lights in the living-room, and I found Al there with Thorne. Al was quite at ease in a comfortable chair, but Thorne was pacing the floor in front of him, talking rapidly.

"I want you to appreciate my position, Captain Branson," he was saying. "Come in, Isabel; you may as well hear this too. I'm as anxious as anyone to have this matter cleared up. I can't claim that Mr. Murdock was a friend of mine, but I have as much respect for his rights as any man's, and if he was deliberately shot, I want to see his murderer brought to justice.

"But my wife and I are practically innocent bystanders. We know nothing about this terrible thing; we have no part in it. We don't wish to be dragged into it any further. My own position would be jeopardized by any publicity."

Al rose rather abruptly.

"I understand you perfectly, Mr. Emory," he said. "I can assure you I will do everything consistent with the public interest to keep you from being involved any further than you already are. More than that I cannot do."

"Thank you," said Thorne, and sat down heavily. He was beginning to perspire. I didn't entirely blame him.

"I won't trouble you any more tonight, Mr. Emory. I'm taking Miss Marsh home. Do you mind if I stop in the library a moment?"

Thorne waved a pudgy hand.

"Go ahead. Help yourself. Good night."

Al took my arm and steered me out of the living-room.

"What did you find out?" he asked, as he led me into the library. There was a heavy green plush curtain over the doorway, and he drew it over as soon as he had found the light switch.

"Al, please, I want to get as far away from this whole business as I can. I don't really think I like these people."

"Is that, as it sounds, an understatement?"

"It is, emphatically. If I were as candid as the younger generation, I think I'd start calling Joan a few four-letter names—or rather, five-letter, if you know what I mean. And I earnestly hope you don't."

"Save the invective. What did you learn?"

"Well, to make it all plain, Joan intended to try blackmail and bribery on Frank tonight, and only Thorne's unexpected return stopped her. And the governess, Miss Ayers, is apparently 'that way' about Frank, and was politely allowing herself to be bribed into silence, or she might have wrecked everything for the Emories. And finally, Murdock was a wolf—and I mean wolf. Pretty picture, isn't it?"

"Isabel, you're altogether too nice to appreciate how commonplace all that is. It happens more often than you'd believe. Perhaps I'm a little disillusioned. But I know that."

"I know it too. But I still don't really like it."

"Well, give me the details. Wait a minute. There's a radio over there. That will cover our voices. There. Now tell me."

I repeated Joan's conversation as well as I could, with a reservation now and then, while the radio played Mexican music from Tijuana and seemed utterly out of place.

"It looks," he said finally, "as if we ought to pay more attention to the sullen Miss Ayers. Isabel, you have a knack for these things, a funny twist in your mind that seems to clear your vision. What do you think of the whole case?"

I had been afraid he'd ask that.

"Al, please. There's no evidence; nothing. Anything I'd say would be guesswork. Oh, don't ask me that!"

"Why not? Is it as bad as that?"

I sat down on the arm of a big sofa.

"Yes, it's as bad as that."

I will say for him that he hesitated then. For a while he looked over the titles of books in the shelves, his back toward me. Then he turned slowly, and his eyes were very friendly but very unrelenting.

"Tell me," he urged. "I know it's only an idea, and I won't take it too seriously."

"There have been one or two things, Al—funny little discrepancies. For instance, when Thorne told me he wouldn't go out into the garden to look for that intruder. And yet he had just been out there, evidently doing exactly that. The fact that he didn't see anyone in that dark doorway, and yet Frank must have, or he wouldn't have said, 'Good Lord, don't,' the way he did. Little things like that. And the curious way the murderer knew Frank would be here tonight . . ."

"He could have followed him."

"He could have, of course. But it was awfully lucky, wasn't it, that the one door he could use should be open?"

"Isabel, what are you driving at?"

"Turn up that radio, will you?"

The plaintive melody of a Mexican love song filled the room.

"Now, what is it?"

"Al, what if Thorne Emory shot him himself?"

He blinked slowly. "Go on," he said. "I don't think I quite expected you to say that. But go on."

"Well," I continued rapidly, because now that I had started I wanted to get it over with quickly, "he could have, couldn't he? He had every reason to be afraid of what Frank could do to him. No matter what he says or Joan says, it looks from where I'm standing as if Frank would have had a pretty strong case when he brought that suit into court. And then Thorne came home to-night and found Frank with Joan.

"Don't you see how he'd feel? Joan hated him too, terribly. But he could bring harm to both of them. And it would have been so easy, if Thorne had a gun with him. All he had to do was to shoot Frank, and then call the police. He's an important man. He might have hoped to use his influence to hush it up. He *did* try to do that; you know he did."

"Yes. He tried hard. You mean, then, that there wasn't any man in the doorway at all? That when Murdock cried out, 'Don't!' he was yelling at Thorne?"

"That's about it. When I told him I'd seen a man outside, Thorne simply jumped at the chance to make use of it. And when he went out to look for the man, he carried the gun out with him and dropped it in the underbrush."

"I see. Would anyone have seen him when he shot Murdock?" I shook my head.

"No, I don't think so. Remember, he especially told Joan to go to her room. She didn't come out until she heard the shot. And he had no idea I was in the living-room. Even the light was out in there."

"Did you smell cordite, gunpowder, or anything?" Al asked suddenly.

"Yes. Now that I think of it, the hall had a strong odor of it."

"Well," Al remarked, "it could have come from the library too, I guess. But if all this happened, then who was the man in the garden?"

"I don't know. It might just have been a prowler. Or somebody who came with Frank, and was just wandering around outside, waiting for him."

"Murdock came in a tan Ford sedan," said Al. "It's parked out on the street now. He's got a Texas license tag on it, and the registration is in Frank Murdock's name. So if anybody came with Frank, he left without waiting for him."

"He may have looked in the window and seen the body, and then run," I suggested.

"Maybe." Al sounded very unconvinced. "Look, Isabel, your theory is interesting, and it fits the facts pretty well. But there's something wrong with it. Take the motive, for one thing. You're suggesting that Thorne Emory killed Murdock to avoid being dragged into a messy alienation suit. I'll admit it's a good motive, and one I'd accept, if it weren't for one thing. Look *where* Frank Murdock was killed. Do you think the Emories would be any better off mixed up in a messy murder case than if they were involved in an alienation suit? I'd call that leaping from the frying pan into the fire.

"Now, if Murdock had been found dead in his own apartment, I'd have arrested Thorne Emory long ago. But as long as the murder occurred here, without any steps being taken to cover it up, I just don't believe it. It was much too careless a murder for a cautious man like Thorne Emory to commit. Remember how careful he was to avoid trouble from Doris Ayers, long before the trouble broke? That's his style, not this."

I sighed with deep relief.

"I'm so glad, Al. You're right, of course. I should have seen that, too. But it does look so simple."

"I'm afraid, Isabel, we'll find it isn't so very simple after all. I think there are a lot of curious angles we haven't even suspected yet. The Ayers angle, for instance. I'd like to talk to her again. Do you think you'd mind waiting long enough for that? Then I promise I'll drive home with you."

"All right. I'm not in that much of a hurry. And I'm curious about her, Al. She's such a peculiar woman."

"Fine. You stay with me, and we'll talk to her together. Try your intuition on her."

He rang a buzzer on the wall, and we waited.

## Chapter IX

DORIS AYERS was not pleased to see me sitting in the library with the Captain, when she came in eventually. Her face was sullen and her eyes dark and brooding. The slightest look of displeasure wrinkled her forehead, but she sat down quietly enough, with a certain admirable poise, for what she must have known would be an ordeal.

"I have to ask you a few questions, Miss Ayers," Al began, "if you don't mind. I'll try not to keep you long."

She folded stubby fingers in her lap, and inclined her head. She sat opposite both of us, but she shifted her position so that she was addressing Al, and subtly ignoring me.

"I have your name as Doris Ayers; is that right?"

"Yes."

"Where are you from, Miss Ayers?"

"I was born in Ohio. I've worked in New York and on Long Island, mostly, since I was quite young."

"As a governess?"

"Usually. Once I tried secretarial work, but my shorthand was too poor. I had to give it up."

"When did you begin to work for Mrs. Emory?"

"It was about a year ago."

"How did you happen to take the position?"

"Mr. Emory engaged me. I had been with a family in Connecticut, friends of his. Their daughter was older than Miss Elaine, and the family had decided to send her away to school. Since I was to be free, Mr. Emory suggested that I come to take care of Elaine."

"I see. That was some time before Mrs. Emory obtained her divorce from Mr. Murdock?"

"Yes. Several months. I believe that Mrs. Emory had already begun to make plans to go to Reno, and the colored nurse she had at the time was timid about going so far from her home." She flashed a fleeting smile. "She was sure there were wild Comanches in Reno. At any rate, I took the job, and after several months we went to Nevada."

"You mean you went with Mrs. Murdock and her daughter?"

She hesitated just a second, and her mouth twitched into a scornful arch.

"Yes," she said briefly.

"Was Mr. Emory a member of the party?"

She nodded. "Mrs. Murdock lived in a small house she had rented. Mr. Emory stayed at a hotel. But he handled most of the business for her, hired her lawyers and so on."

"I understand that Mr. Murdock was also there at the time."

"He was. He came a week or so after we did."

"Did he make any attempt to see Mrs. Murdock?"

"I wouldn't know," she said, and her eyes flashed defiance.

"But he did see Elaine, didn't he?"

"Since Mrs. Emory seems to have told you that, I don't suppose there's any reason for me to deny it. He met us on the street one day. I'm sure the meeting was not accidental. He was waiting at the corner at about the time I usually took Elaine for a walk.

"After that he met us almost every day. Elaine was very fond of him, and he often bought her little toys or presents. When Mrs. Murdock discovered that, she scolded me, and took the presents away from Elaine. After that we were careful to hide them."

"You didn't think you were being disloyal to Mrs. Murdock by doing that?" Al asked, frowning at her. She stared back at him, unmoved.

"I probably was. However, I was engaged to look after Elaine. And I considered it very unwise to try to build up ill-feeling toward her own father. The effect upon her in after years would be apt to be very bad indeed. I couldn't possibly make Mrs. Murdock understand that. She is rather self-centered. I'm sorry if I seem disloyal. I'm trying to be honest."

"Are you quite sure, Miss Ayers, that the real reason you disobeyed Mrs. Murdock's orders wasn't that you were attracted to Mr. Murdock yourself?"

Her face flushed with resentment. Her blunt fingers were clasped more tightly in her lap.

"I considered him a very pleasant, considerate person," she said, with forced calmness. "It's likely that I considered him on the wrong end of a dirty deal, too." She held up her hand to keep Al from interrupting. "I know you'll say I had no business to think anything about it. Probably I hadn't. But I couldn't help it. I thought Mrs. Murdock was being grossly unfair, and I still do." She shrugged. "That's that."

"Did you know Mr. Murdock was staying here in Los Angeles?" She paused for quite a while before she answered that.

"Yes," she said finally. "I have taken Elaine out for rides with him. And," she added quickly, "Mrs. Emory doesn't know about that either."

She must have been prepared for Al's next question, because her reply came almost before it was asked.

"Would it be incorrect if I suggested that sometimes you used Elaine merely as an excuse to see——?"

"It certainly would! There was nothing between Mr. Murdock and myself. I admired him, and felt sorry for him. I like Elaine. If you read anything more into it, you're wrong—absolutely wrong."

Al dropped that line at once.

"But you have seen enough of Mr. Murdock to know whether he had any attachments, no doubt."

I think Al's persistence had begun to rattle her. She was not so calm, not so assured as she had been; and her answers now were not so carefully considered.

"You couldn't blame a man for turning to other women, could you, if he was married to one who gave him nothing but contempt and the cold shoulder? I think he was too honorable a man, or he'd have divorced her years ago. God knows, he had enough evidence!"

Her flat, bovine face was scarlet with anger.

"You personally knew of another woman, then?"

"What if I do? I don't know who she is," she said hastily. "Don't even ask me! I believe I knew Mr. Murdock well enough to know that there was nothing dishonorable or indiscreet—Oh, I won't say anything more about that. You've no right to ask me, and I don't have to answer. That would only be an opinion, anyway. Is that all you wanted to know?"

"By no means," said Al quietly, and motioned her back into her chair. "Did the Emories tell you about the suit for alienation of affections which Mr. Murdock intended to bring?"

"They discussed it, yes." Her caution had returned, and her color had faded again.

"Did they urge you to testify for them?"

"No," she replied, with that odd little scornful smile. "I think they were more anxious to keep me from testifying. I'm afraid my evidence would have been fatal to the defense."

"Did they offer you any inducement at all not to testify?"

"No. I wouldn't have accepted any, either. For Elaine's sake, I doubt if I would have gone on the stand, though. It wouldn't have been right to saddle her with any scandal, would it?"

Al looked at me, and shook his head slowly. I wondered what he was thinking, wondered if the enigma of Doris Ayers was clearing up at all in his mind as it was in mine. Suddenly I felt terribly sorry for her, torn between her loyalties and her much stronger desires, a woman strong enough to face any situation of her own creating, but too uncertain to avoid entanglement in others. I'm afraid Al, on the other hand, saw in her nothing but a woman trying desperately to cover up a shoddy love affair with her employer's ex-husband. I determined to talk to him about it.

He cleared his throat, and went on with him questions.

"Miss Ayers, I want you to tell me about this evening. What you, and everyone else, did from—say—supper time on."

"Very well," she agreed, her poise almost completely restored. "We had supper—and it was supper, not dinner—at about six-thirty. The Emories don't usually dine until seven, but it was the cook's night off, and Sarah, the upstairs maid, had prepared a cold supper, which they ate early. I, naturally, ate with them. About seven, or shortly afterwards, Mr. Emory went out. As soon as he had gone, Mrs. Emory told me to take Elaine upstairs, to read to her for a while and get her to bed early.

"She sometimes did that when she was expecting company, to get Elaine out of the way. Other times we'd go to the movies, but we'd been last night, and Mrs. Emory was very strict about going twice in succession. But she made it very plain she wanted Elaine kept away."

"Did you know Mr. Murdock was coming?"

"No. I—I had no idea until I saw his—his body." For a moment her lips quivered and I thought she was going to cry.

"Very well; you read to the child until when?"

"It was just before Miss Marsh arrived. She was sleepy, and I hadn't any trouble getting her quiet for the night as I do some evenings, early as it was. Then I went down to the kitchen, and helped Sarah finish up the dishes. I didn't leave the kitchen until we heard the shot and both of us went to the dining-room door to see what was wrong."

"Did Sarah leave the kitchen during that time?"

"Only twice. Once to open the door for Miss Marsh. The second time to let Mr. Murdock in."

"Did she tell you who was calling?"

She shook her head.

"Sarah had never seen Mr. Murdock before. The Emories engaged her from an agency here after they arrived. She only told me that a gentleman had come. He evidently didn't give his name."

"Where were you when Mr. Emory returned?"

"In the kitchen, talking to Sarah."

"What time was that?"

"I don't know, exactly. Around eight-thirty. At any rate, it was about ten minutes before we heard the shot."

"And you were with Sarah then? I suppose she could confirm that?"

"Well, as a matter of fact, I had gone upstairs to see if Elaine was still sleeping just before then. I mean, after Mr. Emory arrived. And if I remember rightly, Sarah had carried the trash out to the incinerator. But I came down the back steps almost at once, and Sarah came in from outside about the same time. We both heard the shot, and ran into the dining-room."

"I see. Well," Al said, and stood up, "I think that's about all, Miss Ayers. Thank you. Good night."

She rose too, and murmured a low, "Good night." She left the room without looking at me.

## *Chapter* X

A L INSISTED on driving home with me, after that, even though his own car was parked outside the Emories' house. I don't know what he expected to happen to me, whether he was afraid that the man I had seen in the grounds had recognized me and might still be hanging around, or whether he thought some sort of reaction might set in and I would become hysterical on the way home. But he took the wheel and drove to my house, with Green following in his car, and, once there, came in with me and waited while I turned on my lights.

"I'd suggest," he said solicitously, "that you take a good stiff drink, and get some sleep. You've had a tough evening."

"Everybody I've met all day has handed me Scotch and sodas, Al," I retorted, "and I've had all I want. I spent the afternoon with Cora Cottrell, and you know what her idea of hospitality is. What I will do is to fix myself a glass of warm milk, and read in bed awhile. That will take my mind off things."

"Fine. You're sure you're all right here? Being alone in a big house isn't any fun, you know."

"Al, I'm not alone. Fern's here, and there's Slats, the dog, and besides, I'm getting used to being alone since Web got married."

He put his hands on my shoulders gently, and looked at me with a sort of pleading look.

"You know, I'm rather fond of you, Isabel, and I wouldn't want anybody fooling around here, thinking you knew too much."

"They couldn't think that. I don't know a thing," I said sharply. But I was flattered, and pleased. "Now, don't worry."

"All right. I won't. But when you wake up and realize you're much too attractive a woman to be living in lonely spinsterhood, I'm going to have a long talk with you."

He kissed me lightly on the forehead, and left. For a few moments, after I heard him drive away in his car, the house did seem large, and dark, and lonely. It would have been nice, having someone there with me, fussing around getting glasses out of the kitchen cabinet, taking his shoes off for the night, perhaps whistling to himself, or doing something homey and domestic while I heated that milk.

Well, it lay with me, I knew. And I couldn't make up my mind. At any age, though I'm no septuagenarian, it isn't easy to make the compromise and readjustments that marriage involves. Unless you are desperately in love. And I wasn't altogether sure I was.

I went into the kitchen, my lips shut with determination, and heated my milk for myself. Afterwards I selected a book to read. I studiously avoided the two romances I'd taken from the lending library that morning, and chose instead a biography of Columbus that Cora Cottrell had lent me.

And in spite of Al's fears, or doubts, I dropped off to sleep almost before I knew it, and slept soundly, without alarms or disturbance.

But Al, as he told me the next day, had not gone to bed for hours. He had Green drive him to the apartment near La Brea, where Frank had been staying, to continue his investigations there.

I saw the place afterwards, and can describe it fairly well. It was in a court, a small white bungalow like eleven others arranged around a square of lawn, and its flimsy walls were brightened with bougainvillea. A gateway led into the court, and to the parking sheds that joined each house to the next like a series of Siamese twins.

It must have been after twelve before they arrived; but they found a light burning in the bungalow where Frank had lived. Al rang the doorbell, and presently a man in his shirtsleeves answered, a little irritable at having been disturbed so late.

"Does Mr. Frank Murdock live here?" Al asked him.

"Yes," the man said ungraciously. "He hasn't come in yet. I don't know when to expect him. What do you want?"

"May we come in?" asked Al. "I'm Captain Branson, of the Sheriff's office."

The man held the door open, then, puzzled and, Al thought,

worried. He was a man of thirty-five or six, short, with a ruddy face, and very black, thick hair that had a natural wave. His eyes were a dark brown, with the bright, surprised look of a dog's.

"Who are you?" Al asked, as he and Green followed him into the little sitting-room. There was mostly wicker furniture in it, in the painted, primitive style they sometimes call California mission, and inexpensive chintz curtains. A portable radio stood on an untidy table, and the evening paper lay scattered on the floor.

"I'm James Murdock, Frank's brother. Is Frank in any trouble?"

He indicated seats for them with a careless wave of his hand, and began to pack a pipe with tobacco. Al said he seemed nervous, and very ill at ease.

"Do you live here with him, Mr. Murdock?"

James nodded, the match to his pipe bowl. He blew out smoke and answered:

"Yes, Frank and I have been sharing this place for two or three weeks, until we can find a better place. But what's wrong?"

But Al still did not answer directly.

"Have you been here all evening, Mr. Murdock?" he asked, looking around the room.

"No, I came in about an hour ago." He glanced at Al, and amplified his reply. "I'd been to a movie."

"You understand I'm forced to asked these questions—matter of routine. What time did you go out?"

James was more puzzled than ever, but he answered without hesitation.

"At about seven, or seven-thirty. I didn't notice. After Frank and I had finished supper. We do our own cooking here most of the time."

"And what theater did you go to?"

James gave him the name of a theater in the neighborhood. "But I'm in the dark about this, Captain. Would you mind telling me what's happened?"

Having given James a few moments to worry, and a chance to blurt out any guilty knowledge if he had had any (a method of approach I've noticed in other members of the police, and dislike thoroughly; it gives me a creepy, guilty feeling every time they try it), he told James the news, and watched his reaction.

"Your brother was shot and killed tonight. I'm sorry to have to bring you news like this, Mr. Murdock."

"Good Lord!" James, who had been standing by the table, sat down suddenly on the arm of a chair. "What happened to him, Captain Branson? Sorry—this is pretty much of a shock to me."

"I was hoping you could help me. We don't know yet who shot him."

"Was it accidental? I mean, a stray bullet or something? No, I guess not, or you wouldn't have asked me where I was."

"He was deliberately murdered, Mr. Murdock."

"It can't believe it!" James' pipe had gone out, but he still held it in his hand, forgotten. "Where did this happen?"

Again Al ignored him, anxious to get information, not give it.

"Do you know if he was going anywhere in particular tonight?"

James replied very cautiously.

"Why, yes, I believe he did have an appointment for around eight," he said, and waited for Al's next question.

"An appointment where?"

James looked uncomfortable.

"I'd rather not say, unless I have to," he protested. "I'm not trying to be close-mouthed, you understand. That appointment was his own business—*unless* it was at the appointment that he was shot. If that's what happened, of course I'll tell you right away. I—Good Lord, I hope you understand me, Captain. I don't want to get into trouble or anything."

Al is used to the evasions of witnesses, and wise enough to know they are not necessarily guilty evasions.

"I see your point, Mr. Murdock," he said, not without sympathy. "And, since you feel that way, I think you'd better tell me."

"I get it. All right, he went to call on his former wife."

"Thanks. He left here, then, to go there?"

"Yes. Just about the same time I did. In his car. I have a Ford coupé of my own, and I went to the movies in that. I haven't seen him since."

"Do you know why he was calling on her?"

"We discussed it, yes. She had sent for him, you see, to talk over some—well, some business. He didn't want to go, because he couldn't see that any good would come of it. I gather you know what the business was?" he said inquiringly.

"Yes, Mr. Emory discussed that with us rather thoroughly."

James sighed, and seemed somewhat relieved.

"Well, I'll tell you that I didn't like anything about the business," he declared. "I've been trying, ever since we got here, to knock the idea out of his thick skull. But Frank was stubborn as an ox. Always was. If he took a dislike to anybody, he really disliked them. He hated Thorne Emory's guts. I didn't blame him for that; but he wasn't making things any better by suing him.

"I tried to tell him that. I tried to make him see that if he brought the thing into court he'd only make himself look like a sap or a heel or both. Anyway, it wouldn't do him any good."

"He stood to gain half a million dollars if he won," Al pointed out. "A man would do a lot for that."

James frowned at his pipe. His dark eyes were shrewd and bright.

"I know. I'm not saying Frank didn't like money, too, mainly because he'd never had any. But look who Emory is. The man could hire the best lawyers in the country, while the best Frank could do was to go to a person like Post, who'd take the case on a gamble, and start raising all the stink he could to play for a settlement out of court. If Emory held out, how did Frank know he'd win his case? Post may be up to plenty of tricks, but Emory's attorneys would know their law, *and* the trick. It was a dumb play, *I* thought, and I told him so."

"Sure," said Al succinctly. "What it amounted to was legalized blackmail."

"That's about it." James got up and began hunting among the debris on the table top for a pipe cleaner. "But Frank was hopped up. He said Emory had stolen his wife and his child, and he couldn't forget it. You couldn't make him see sense."

"Why did he go over there tonight?"

"He figured Joan, his wife, would offer to make a settlement. You see, Frank figured he had them where he wanted them. He had enough evidence to win the case hands down, *he* thought. He told me he wouldn't take a cent less than two hundred thousand to call it off. And if they kicked about that, he'd walk out and let them stew awhile." An idea struck him, and he fell into silence, considering it. His whole expression changed to thunderstruck amazement.

"Great Scott, don't tell me Thorne Emory shot him!" he exclaimed. "He wouldn't be that big a fool!"

"Exactly what we think, Mr. Murdock. By the way, had you planned to offer testimony if this matter had come to court?"

"Me? Yes, I suppose so. I'm not certain, but I suppose I'd have supported Frank. I didn't like it, but, after all, the man's my own brother. I'd have told what I knew, which wasn't much, except that Frank tried to be a good husband to her, and to support her. That was true. He wasn't much as a money-maker, but I know he loved his wife very deeply, until she turned away from him."

"I've heard that he wasn't always faithful to her," Al said casually. He saw James flush a little.

"That's not true, except in a sense. Look, I know Frank pretty darn well. He was a good-looking kid. Too damn good-looking for his own good. It turned his head when he was younger. Sure, he played around when he was young. Why not? But after he married, he tried to settle down. But something went wrong; I don't know what. Maybe she got tired of trying to live on nothing. Maybe she never loved him at all, and felt sorry she'd let Emory slip when she could have had him. I don't like to call names or anything, but she always struck me as a pretty shallow dish. I don't think she ever loved anybody. Frank swept her off her feet, but it didn't last. It didn't last longer than tomorrow's hangover.

"A man can't take that forever. Frank had been popular with his crowd and he was used to women liking him. If his wife turned sour on him, what would you expect? Maybe he did begin to play around again. I say it wouldn't have happened if she'd stuck to him. The right woman would have helped Frank make something out of himself. Joan wasn't the right woman."

"Was there any particular woman in whom he was interested?" Al asked. He tried to make that question casual, too, hoping that James' garrulous streak would continue. But he pulled in his horns, as Al expressed it, like a garden snail tickled with a twig.

"No!" he scowled. Al had interrupted his thoughts rudely. For a while he had been reminiscing, almost as if he were trying, somehow, to formulate in his own mind his feelings toward his brother. He showed no grief, but he was, on the other hand, not callous. It was rather the resigned acceptance of an unpleasant fact. When Al told me about it later, I thought of Macbeth's philosophic comment when they told him of his wife's death. "She should have died hereafter. There would have been a time for such a word."

But now he roused himself to an emphatic denial of Al's suggestion.

"I certainly don't know of a single person Frank cared about that way," he added with finality. Al thought he was lying.

"You couldn't suggest anyone who—?"

"I said I couldn't. I don't know of anyone; and I'm quite sure I would have if there had been anyone."

"Did Doris Ayers ever visit him here?"

"Doris Ayers? I don't know any Doris Ayers."

"His daughter's nurse."

"Oh, that one. Yes, she dropped in with Elaine once, I think, or maybe twice." A sudden smile curved his lips. "You don't suspect him of having been smitten with the dusky Doris, do you? He wanted to see his daughter."

"Miss Ayers, nevertheless, was very much in love with your brother," Al told him. He digested that a moment.

"That's possible. I hadn't thought about it, but the one time I saw her she did have that look in her eye, now that I recall it. But I don't think Frank even knew what she looked like."

"You said your brother had evidence," Al said then, taking a new line, "that would win his case for him. In what form was that evidence?"

"There were—there was very little in tangible evidence, if that's what you mean, as far as I know. Post has what there is. I think Frank had a copy of a bill from a jeweler for a bracelet and a few things like that. Most of the evidence, though, was in the form of depositions, and the promises of witnesses."

"And who were those witnesses?"

"Ayers was one of them. Joan's cook in the East. The jeweler and his assistant. There were depositions from tradesmen showing Emory had paid her bills for several years, and a few dressmaking people. All the usual sort of thing."

"Did your brother make any contribution to his wife's support during the time Mr. Emory was supposed to be paying her bills?"

"Supposed to be? He was," James said, with a grunt of decision. "As for Frank, he sent her two hundred a month every time he was away. When he was at home, naturally he paid all the bills, or believed he did. I know that for a fact."

"How do you know it?"

"Well—" He reddened, and remembered his pipe which he had dropped after stuffing a cleaner into it. He began jabbing at the cleaner self-consciously. "I—I saw the checks."

"Was your brother living with you during all that time?"

"No. Hardly ever. I was in New York, and he—" He stopped suddenly and looked at Al, realizing what he had said.

"Then how does it happen you saw the checks to Mrs. Murdock?"

"Oh, well, you might as well have it. I sent them myself. Frank was making just about enough to keep himself going. I—I helped him out now and then."

Al was certainly not content to let it go at that.

"I understand you to say you practically supported your brother's wife, Mr. Murdock. Why did you do that? You surely weren't under any obligation to do so."

"No. No, and I had no love for Joan," he admitted. "Look, see if I can make you see it. Frank was my brother, my younger brother. We were orphans. I'd sort of taken care of him and—well, I guess it got to be a habit, that's all."

"Two hundred a month is a rather expensive habit," remarked Al drily.

James seemed acutely embarrassed.

"Oh, you wouldn't understand, at that! Frank loved that crazy woman he married. He wanted to make a go of the marriage, but it took time for him to make himself independent and able to take care of her. He'd never done much work in his life. With enough money coming in, he thought Joan would be satisfied. In a way it was a sort of a loan on my part, not to be paid back in cash. Hell, can't you see all I wanted to do was to give the poor kid a break? My income could take it. I haven't Emory's gold mine, but my papers are making money, and I don't want much for myself. I didn't miss it." He shrugged and gave up, with a last glance at Al's immobile features. He threw the pipe back on the table.

"Where's Frank now?" he asked.

Al told him. He nodded.

"You'll let me know about when I can arrange for the funeral, won't you?"

"Yes, of course. Is there any other help you can give us, Mr. Murdock? It's our business, you know, to find out who killed your brother."

"Sure. I know. If I could help, I would. If you asked me, I'd say Emory did it. But I guess you know best."

"By the way," Al put in, as he got up to go, "you didn't go to the movies with anybody?"

"No. I haven't been here long enough to get to know many people. I went alone."

"Did anybody see you there, who could identify you?"

"I'm afraid not. I don't go to that theater often. But—wait a minute—if you're trying to check on my being there. I might help you. I parked too near an alley intersection, and I found this parking ticket on the car when I came out."

He fished around in a worn pigskin wallet, and handed Al a slip of paper. Al glanced at it curiously. It was a notice to appear at the nearest precinct station and post collateral on a charge of improper parking. The place where this occurred was stated: it was half a block from the theater and the time was given as eight-twenty. The signature of the officer making the charge was scrawled on the bottom.

Al made a note of the data and handed it back to him.

"That seems to check up," Al remarked.

"I don't suppose you could do anything about fixing that up for me," James began, and added, when he saw Al slowly shake his head, "No—I was afraid of that."

"That's all for the moment," Al said. "But be sure and stay here, or let us know immediately if you leave this address. And you'd better not leave town."

"I won't."

"And while I'm here, I'll take along any papers or letters belonging to your brother. They might contain information."

"Of course." He crossed to a small desk and pulled open the drawer. "They're all in there. Not many, at that. That stuff on the left is mine."

Al ran through all of it, to be sure of missing nothing. A few minutes later, with a package of letters in his coat pocket, he took his departure. At the gate he nodded to a man who seemed to be strolling by. The man touched the brim of his hat.

Al drove home, then.

## Chapter XI

THE NEXT day was a trying one for me in more ways than one. I awoke early, as I usually do, and had my breakfast in bed. Fern brought it in to me with the morning paper, with her eyes almost falling out of her head. She has been with

me for years, and had known Joan in the old days. I could see at
once that she had sneaked a look at the paper before she
brought it in.

When she had placed the tray, she spread the paper out over my
knees and stood waiting, which was unlike her.

"What is it, Fern?" I asked.

"That Mr. Murdock, Miss Isabel. Was you there when that
happened?"

"Yes. I was there."

"Golly!" she exclaimed. "Seems like nothing but trouble comes
to them people. You'd better stay away from the house."

"I'm certainly going to, from now on," I promised. She was
still shaking her head when she left the room. I opened the paper,
skipping all the harrowing headlines from the Pacific on the front
page, and found the murder on page two. Only the crisis of Bataan
could have placed it there.

But it was a disappointing account. When I considered all
the sensational possibilities in that story, I was surprised at the
restraint shown. Not that it wasn't bad enough. But the reporters
had not got hold of the alienation suit at all, and, mercifully, I
had not been identified yet. I knew what would happen when I
was. I had been through that before. They made all they could,
though, of Frank being killed in his successor's house, with refer-
ences to the divorce that just missed being dangerously close
to libel.

There would be more in the evening papers, I knew. The early
edition had come out too soon to contain more than the merest
outline. I rang for Fern to warn her against reporters, and she
came in, more excited than before.

"That Mrs. Emory's nurse is outside in the living-room," she
said. "She wants you should go over to the house right away. I
told her you wasn't up yet."

"Nurse?" I asked, surprised. "You mean Miss Ayers?"

"Yes'm," said Fern, exuding disapproval from every pore.
"Shall I tell her you're indisposed or something?"

"Yes—no, wait." All my resolutions began to melt in the face
of my curiosity and uneasiness. "Ask her to wait a moment.
I'll be right out."

I pushed my breakfast tray aside, and drew on a negligee. I
found Miss Ayers, standing stiff and straight, in the living-room,
drawing a pair of gloves again and again through her fingers. She

was wearing the same dark blue dress she had worn the night before, so plain it might almost have been a uniform, relieved only by a white organdy collar. Her face was pale, and she looked as if she had been crying. There was no friendliness in her expression as she turned to me.

"Good morning, Miss Marsh," she said formally. "I'm sorry to disturb you so early. But Mrs. Emory sent me, and asked me to beg you to come over to see her at once. She insists it's most important."

"Very well," I replied. "I'll come. Have you a car?"

"Yes. The Rolls. Mrs. Emory would have telephoned you, but she has a fear the phone is tapped, and she wants to talk to you privately."

"Just a moment," I said, and hurried back to my room to dress. I rejoined her in a minute or two, and we drove to the Emory house in complete silence. The one attempt I made at conversation, an inquiry as to how Joan was feeling, met with so curt a reply that I hesitated to try again.

Sarah opened the door for us, and asked me to go directly upstairs. I hurried up the dim stairway, wondering what had made her send for me with such urgency.

That it was urgent one look at her confirmed. There was no pretense of shock or grief in Joan's wan face, lined with unhappiness. She was crying without restraint, and without trying to conceal it. She had not even bothered to fix her hair. She was propped against the pillows in the soft bed, tired-looking and old.

She held her arms out to me like an unhappy child. There was nothing I could do but pat her for a moment, and murmur sympathetically. A stone statue could have done no less.

"What's wrong, Joany? Tell me, what's the matter?"

But sympathy, as usual, was the wrong treatment. She began to sob against my shoulder, and it was a long time before I could quiet her enough to talk to her.

"It's Thorne," she finally managed to say. "Oh, Isabel, they've taken him to prison!"

"Thorne!" I cried, and held her away, staring into her eyes incredulously.

"They've arrested him for murder, Isabel. They've taken him down to jail."

"I don't believe it, Joan. You must be wrong."

"No. No. I tell you they did. That Captain Branson came at

eight o'clock and took him along. It's too awful, Isabel! Thorne and I hated Frank; I don't pretend we didn't. But he didn't shoot him. You know he wouldn't do that!"

"Of course he wouldn't," I declared. "But what on earth made the Captain do that, Joan? Did they find out anything new that made them think he might have?"

"I don't know," she said, dabbing at her eyes with a wisp of a handkerchief. "I didn't see him except when he said goodbye. And he didn't know, either. The police hadn't even been here since you left last night."

"I can't understand it," I said thoughtfully. "Al seemed so sure last night Thorne hadn't done it. I wonder what could have happened." A thought occurred to me, and I tried to explain it to Joan tactfully, and in such a way that it would not add to her distress. "It could have been the gun. They might have traced it. Tell me, Joan, did Thorne have a gun like that?"

"Like what?"

"It was a Colt .25 automatic, I think they said. Had Thorne one?"

"No. He didn't own a gun. As far as I know he never owned one."

"Then it wasn't that." I thought over everything that had been said the night before, as well as I could remember it, but I could not see anything that would give even a hint as to why they had arrested him.

"Isabel, you know that Captain. Please do what you can, won't you? This will be too awful for Thorne.

"I'll do what I can, Joan," I promised. "But it may not be much. I can't interfere with the police."

"But you can help them to understand, Isabel," she insisted, holding tight to the edge of my skirt, as if she expected to see me fly away at any instant. "You know Thorne. You can help that Captain—what's his name?—you can help him find out who did it. I know you can. I know how you helped him once before. Alice told me about that. *Please*, Isabel, do something."

I sighed, and reached for the telephone, an instrument in white plastic that stood on the dressing table. There seemed to be a phone in almost every room of that house.

"What are you going to do?" Joan asked.

"I'm going to call Al, and find out what *did* happen," I said, and dialled a number. She watched me with reddened eyes.

"Hello," I said, when I finally located him after trying half a dozen places. "Al? This is Isabel."

"Good morning," he said cheerfully. Sleep all right?"

"Yes. Very well. Listen, Al. I'm at the Emories'. I've been talking to Joan. Is it true that you've arrested Thorne for murder?"

"Did she tell you that?" he asked.

"Yes. Is it true?"

"Not exactly. Can she hear you, if I talk softly?"

"I don't think so," I replied, moving to a chaise longue, and drawing the phone cord with me. "What is it?"

"You know how things stood, Isabel. My personal feeling in the matter doesn't count. If you hadn't just happened to see that figure outside there, I would have been forced to arrest Emory at once, on the evidence. Whoever planned that murder did it thoroughly. He managed it so that Emory looked as guilty as— well, plenty guilty. I don't suppose he even knows that anybody saw him. You were in a dark room, and from outside he'd never realize anyone was in the room at all. Get that?"

"Yes."

"Well, he's our dark horse. For one thing, until we can find him, and prove he exists, the evidence is still all against Emory. I had to take him into custody or lose my job. Even then I only held him for questioning.

"I know it's not comfortable for him, and I hated doing it. But I had to, and in a way it's better for him, and for us. I don't want our man to know he was seen out there. If he finds that out, he'll try to cover up somehow.

"Then there's another thing. Emory wasn't completely frank with me last night. He told me only what he thought was safe. He was so darned scared of notoriety. I've got to know everything he can tell us—for his sake as well as ours. So I have him where he can think it over."

"What do you want to know?"

"Who the other woman is. Emory had evidence he intended to use in court to prove that Frank was having an affair. That wasn't used in the divorce case, you know. Mrs. Murdock got a divorce on the grounds of desertion."

"Oh. I see."

"Tell Mrs. Emory, if she's worried, that we'll release her husband the moment we find one piece of evidence exonerating him."

"Al, did you trace the gun?" I asked anxiously.

"Not yet. I don't believe it was Emory's. There's no record of his having a gun. But I'm not sure yet. Tracing the gun to someone else would certainly be evidence enough to release him, though."

"Were there fingerprints on it?"

"No."

"Thanks. That's all, Al. But I was anxious to know."

"I want to see you later in the day, Isabel. Will you be around?"

"I'll be at home."

I don't think Joan got much out of my end of the conversation, and I wasn't quite sure how much of it he didn't want her to hear. But there had been a message for her, and I delivered it as soon as I hung up.

"Joan, you must stop worrying. They haven't arrested Thorne. He's only down there to answer a few questions."

"Oh, Isabel, you're not lying to me, are you?"

"Of course not! As soon as they find out a few more things he'll be home. So don't you get worked up. Have the police talked to you yet?"

"No," she said. "Thorne got Dr. Avery to examine me and tell them I'm too upset to talk. So I haven't been bothered. You're *sure* he's all right?"

"Of course he is!" I declared, with more conviction than I felt. It seemed to me it was up to Al to find out who the man outside had been and do it quickly. Otherwise Thorne would be in a spot.

I stood up to go.

"What you need is rest, Joan," I said, more kindly than I had spoken the night before. I was beginning to feel sorry for her, and the horrid mess she had got herself into, however much to blame she was. "And you can trust Al Branson absolutely to be thorough, and just, and level-headed. He won't let anything happen to Thorne as long as there's any other possibility. So cheer up. And I'll drop in to see you later, if you like."

"You're a lamb, Isabel," she said, with unusual sincerity. "And please don't think too harshly of me. I've made mistakes, I suppose. But I never meant for anything like this to happen. But it isn't our fault. Honestly it isn't!"

I left her after that, and went downstairs. The house was deathly quiet, with a brooding stillness that was uncomfortable. I was glad to get out of it, to the warm March sunshine and the shining Rolls Royce that was waiting to take me home.

## *Chapter* XII

W HEN I reached home I found that the reporters had arrived in swarms, and were hovering around waiting for the victim to approach. They spotted Joan's car at once, and I had to make the chauffeur drive by and leave me in the alley behind the house. And there one of them was taking pictures of my patio, and cornered me.

There was nothing to do then but capitulate and tell them what I thought it was safe to reveal. Of course they remembered me from the Dodge case, which had been not too long ago for their encyclopedic memories; and the reports in the evening editions gave me almost as much space as the Emories.

I finally got rid of them, as gracefully as I could and tried to isolate myself on the patio. But I couldn't settle down to reading, with my mind wandering away from Columbus and his voyage into the unknown to my own problems. Knitting was no better help, because it not only gave me too much time to think, but, as always, produced in me incredulous speculation on the required anatomy of anyone who might wear socks or a sweater such as I produced. Only a deteriorating mankind could include the lop-shouldered freaks on whom those sweaters would be a good fit.

So I put on old slacks and the wide-brimmed straw hat I wear for gardening, and decided to clear out an unsightly succulent bed that I had inherited intact from the former owner of the house.

I was tugging at an impossibly stubborn and thorny century plant, struggling to dislodge it like a robin with a tenacious worm, when a shadow fell across the bed. I dropped the century plant, which sank back into its favorite hole with a sigh of content, while I rose to my feet hurriedly.

Alice Trent was standing beside me, her cheeks pink from a mixture of emotions.

"Isabel!" she exclaimed. "Leave that idiotic cactus thing, or whatever it is, and talk to me."

I drew off the thick leather gloves I was wearing, and walked with her toward the house.

"You've seen the papers, haven't you?" she asked as we approached it. "About Frank, I mean."

"Yes, I saw them." We reached the terrace and I threw my gloves and a five-pronged instrument that always reminds me of a clutching hand onto the table. Alice dropped down in a big chair without invitation, and clasped her hands in her lap. "Terrible, wasn't it?" I said.

"Isabel, what happened? Just think, we were talking about them only a day or two ago. And then this happens. I can't believe it. You don't think Thorne killed him, do you? My mind just won't grasp it."

Her rich voice was huskier than usual. I thought her eyes looked heavier and weary, but I might have been wrong.

"I hate to talk about it," I told her, as I settled myself on the swing, and reached for my cigarettes. "The papers didn't mention it this morning, but I was there, Alice."

"You were there?" she repeated, startled. "How in the world did that happen? I thought you were supposed to go over next week sometime. Tuesday, wasn't it?"

"Yes. But Joan called me last night and asked me to come over."

"I've wanted to go over all morning, to see if I could help her in any way," she put in, "but Burton's absolutely forbidden me to mix up in it in any way, and I suppose he's right." Burton was Alice's husband, a bulky ex-football player, with a moody disposition and a fiery temper, who seemed to dominate her completely. He is the head of a firm which is manufacturing plane parts now, and has branches here and in the East. But I have always believed that Burton, who is a brilliant man, hopes to give that up as soon as the war situation makes it possible and run for Congress in his home state. He has always played in politics.

I could see, therefore, why he'd want Alice to keep out of the Emories' troubles.

"He's right, of course," I agreed.

"But tell me what happened, Isabel."

I was oddly reluctant, I found. Somehow repeating it all made me feel the horror of it with added force. I must have given her the barest outline, because she pestered me with a hundred questions. I studiously avoided mentioning the man outside, knowing Alice's penchant for gossiping and Al's anxiety to keep that fact quiet.

"The police think Thorne did it, then, don't they?" she said finally. "I can't imagine it. But to do that to poor Frank! Isabel, I'm too distressed for words."

"I don't know that I'd feel too sorry for Frank," I said sharply. "He was going to sue Thorne for half a million dollars, and from what I can discover, he wasn't going to be any too delicate about it. Thorne's reputation wouldn't have been worth a hoot afterwards."

"Well, but Thorne was pretty brazen about stealing Frank's wife, Isabel. You have to admit that."

"Apparently Thorne wasn't the only one who was brazen," I pointed out. "It looks to me as if Frank was having an affair with Elaine's governess, and goodness knows how many other women. There was a girl in El Paso, and Thorne hinted strongly that he knew of a married woman, and he intended to bring out her name during the trial. So Frank wasn't exactly an angel."

Her eyes were wide with what I took to be horror.

"Oh, no! No, he wouldn't do that!"

"He'd have done anything to win his case; you know that. He's that way."

She had dropped her cigarette, and it was burning unnoticed on the tiles of the terrace.

"He wouldn't drag another woman through something like that, Isabel! He couldn't! It would be too cruel."

"You know yourself Thorne isn't the sort to consider other people."

"But there won't be any trial now, will there?"

"No, naturally not."

"Well, all I can say is, if Thorne Emory killed that man, I hope he gets whatever is coming to him! You can't ride rough-shod over the world, Isabel, and get away with it. And don't you believe all that nonsense about the governess. Whatever else anyone might say about Frank, he had discrimination."

She got up abruptly.

"I've got to run along," she said. "I'm doing all the marketing these days, trying to economize."

"I don't blame you. I'm going to put in a Victory garden myself. And, Alice, don't think too much about all this. We know Joan and Thorne and all of them, but they're not intimate friends any more. Just try to forget it. Why don't you and Burton come over for dinner some night and we'll get Cora for bridge?"

"I'd love to, if I can pry Burton lose from his work. He spends most of his time at the plant. He hasn't been home for dinner one night for the past week."

"Well, if he can make it, call me and set a night."

"I will. Goodbye, Isabel. And if I were you I'd stay away from the Emories. You can't touch pitch without getting sticky."

I agreed, as I went to the door with her.

I was glad to see her go. I wanted to be alone for a while, to think.

Because I saw I was in a dilemma, and I didn't know what to do. Alice's visit had shaken me more than she realized. I am, I think, reasonably intelligent, and I can add two and two as well as the next person.

I went back to the century plant and got it loose with one tug, in the mood I was in. For the next twenty minutes I worked furiously, with my mind keeping pace.

For Alice had given herself away as devastatingly as if she had made a full confession. I remembered my talk with her the other day, and the way she had stood up for Frank all the way through it. It hadn't meant much to me then, but in view of what I knew now, it took on a sinister significance. And her remark, so casual at the time, when I had told her Joan was in town: "Does Frank know, I wonder," she had said. To have said that, she must have known Frank was in Los Angeles. And yet she had not told me she knew.

She had just mentioned that Burton was away from home a great deal of the time, busy. Too busy, I thought, to realize what was taking place in his own house. And Alice's expression, when I had told her that Thorne had intended to mention the woman Frank had been seeing, hadn't been one of horror so much as fright. It all added up incriminatingly.

And what a position it put me in! I had promised to help Joan, but to do it, I had to involve another, and a much more sincere friend.

But then I realized that that was hardly true. Joan and Emory must have known very well what I knew. It was up to them, not to me, to bring that matter up.

And instantly I determined that they should not; that I would protect Alice, in every way I could. I suppose, in a way, it was none of my business. But I knew Alice well, and liked her. If she had been indiscreet, I was not going to blame her. I would have thought Alice the last person to be dazzled by Frank, probably because I was so sure she loved Burton. But it is a truism that we probably know least of all about the people we think we know best.

If Burton ever learned anything about it, I wasn't sure what he might do. He is as civilized as any of us, but he has a temper, and more than once I'd suspected that Alice had had unpleasant sessions with him when he was annoyed.

And then I saw that my championship of Alice would bring complications in my association with Al. He wanted the name of the woman in Frank's life; he had even taken Thorne with him in order to learn it. And I knew it, and could tell him, if he ever asked me.

Well, there was the loophole. He had not asked me, and I wouldn't volunteer the information.

I cancelled a lunch date with some friends who knew I was acquainted with the Emories, and spent the afternoon working in the garden, a full-time job these days, now that my Japanese gardener was interned somewhere in the mountains, and I had to share a new man with practically everybody within two blocks. All the time I hoped Al would call, because I was becoming more concerned about Alice by the minute.

It was late afternoon when I finally heard from him.

"I'm driving out to talk to the servants at the Emories," he said over the phone. "Mind if I stop by to see you for a moment or two?"

"No. I'd like it. Is there anything new?"

"A few things."

"Did—did Thorne tell you anything?"

"No. Nothing." I must have sighed without realizing it. "What's the matter, Isabel? You sound relieved. You don't know something *you* haven't told me, do you?"

"Me? No, I was just thinking Joan would be sorry Thorne wasn't coming home." I hoped the lame excuse would satisfy him. "I'll wait for you, Al."

## Chapter XIII

I HAD changed into something less informal by the time Al arrived, to save time. I was due later at Cora Cottrell's for cocktails, and I didn't know how long Al might keep me. I waited for him in the garden, fragrant from the mock-orange blossoms along the side fence. I was afraid, at first, that he would discover how nervous I was, because he is, after all, not blind. But for some reason he did not seem to detect it, though I felt as if I were fluttering like a leaf. Possibly he merely assumed that the joy of seeing him had unnerved me, and for once I was not prone to disillusion him.

He sank into a chair wearily and surveyed the garden with contentment while he slowly lighted a cigarette.

"This is wonderful, Isabel, just sitting here like this for a moment or two," he said. "I don't have time to relax. And as for coming home at night to anything so comfortable—"

I saw what he was getting at in a roundabout way, and steered him away from that subject.

"Any time you want to come out here and pull succulents out of rock-solid adobe, Al, you're more than welcome. Or fertilize the beds. Or do something about snails or those great big grasshoppers that eat, I'm told, ten times their own weight in twenty-four hours. Anyone who thinks all you have to do is to stick a seed in the ground to get flowers in California is crazy. All this charm wasn't achieved by sitting in a chair in the patio."

"I'm good at exterminating parasites and pests, Isabel. I'd better help you sometime."

"Well, help me now," I begged, "by satisfying some of my curiosity. What have you been doing all day?"

He sighed and settled deeper in his chair, as if he didn't even want to talk about it.

"That friend of yours, Thorne Emory," he said, holding out his cigarette and looking at the end of it. "Tough customer. Or oily, maybe. He should have been a lawyer. He's as cautious as one. And you can't ruffle him."

"He hasn't talked yet?"

He pursed his lips and shook his head. "No. And our friend Sherman is getting ready to bring him home. I don't think we can hold him without something concrete."

"Any luck at finding out who the man outside was?"

No. None. I'll tell you one thing," he said. "If he tramped around those paths back of the Emory house much, his trouser legs would have been covered with burs. Ryan spent ten minutes pulling the damn things off his own legs last night. But I can't go around examining everybody's trouser legs—not everybody in Los Angeles. And for all we know it could have been anybody out there. You knew, by the way, didn't you, that Frank **Murdock** had a brother?"

"Yes. James. I know him almost as well as Frank. He's in the East somewhere, I suppose."

"You suppose wrong. He's right here in Hollywood."

I was not so surprised at that as Al expected me to be. James had always been moving around, as long as I could remember.

Al proceeded to tell me then about going to Frank's apartment and meeting James.

"None of that got us much further," he said when he'd finished.

"You didn't think James being here was odd, then?"

"Not particularly."

"And that alibi? You know, Al, that smells fishy. You realize, don't you, that he has a perfect alibi for his car, but not for himself?"

"Oh, yes. That's why the man I left there did a little snooping when James wasn't around. He found the stub of a movie ticket tucked in the upper coat pocket of the suit he had worn that night. It was easy enough to check up at the theater and find out the ticket had been sold just about the time he said he'd gone in. They keep a record of those serial numbers, you know. The number D910485 was printed on both ends of the ticket, so that when the usher tore it in half, the part he threw in his collection box had the number on it, and we could compare it with James' half. He went to the theater all right."

He looked at me with a quizzical smile. "Trying to make a suspect of James, Isabel?"

"No, not exactly. Just skeptical about everybody, I suppose. Do you suppose he had any motive at all?"

"I didn't spot one strong enough to lead to fratricide. He was paying out something like two hundred a month to support Mrs. Murdock, but I have an idea he could have stopped that any time he liked. I'm trying to find out if he did stop after Mrs. Murdock got her divorce."

"You mean blackmail?" I asked.

"Something like that. But if the payments did stop, then there's nothing there. And in any case, Isabel, I have an idea—no more— that James had hopes of cashing in a little on Frank's haul. He told me, you remember, that his payments to Frank were prac- tically a loan. So he actually stands to lose a nice little sum since Frank's dead and the case won't come to trial."

I considered that for a moment.

"You're probably right," I agreed finally.

"Your idea is, isn't it, that everyone's guilty until one of them has been proved individually guilty?" When I nodded, he smiled. "It's not a bad approach, either, Isabel. It's a lot better than getting preconceived notions, and tracking them down while you neglect everything else."

"I don't suspect James," I explained, "mainly because so far there's no reason to. Something may crop up. But, eliminating him, who else is there?"

"So far, nobody at all. If all I've heard about Frank is true, the man outside may have been an irate husband. I don't know whose husband or what husband. And I don't know what else he might have been doing there."

"Well, one thing I'm sure of," I said. "He wasn't a prowler trying to pinch Thorne's new tires. He *tried* to kill Frank. That's what he came there for, and what he intended doing."

"The police surgeon reports that the angle of entry of the bullet is consistent with the shot coming from the door. Frank must have been on the eighth or ninth step from the bottom when he was shot. The bullet entered his heart from a very low angle, grazing his lower rib. Thorne, standing behind him and three or four steps higher, couldn't have shot him unless he lay flat on the steps."

I frowned a little. "That certainly does seem to leave Thorne out of it, doesn't it?"

"Pretty definitely."

"Was there anything in the papers you took from his desk?"

"Not a blasted thing. If he kept any love letters, he hid them or put them in a safe deposit box. The only thing I could find was bills, and not many of those, a copy of his income tax blank—he had an income of about thirty-five hundred from salary and commissions. There were one or two personal letters from friends in the East or in Texas. Nothing useful at all. But I think Post, his attorney, has all the documents for the alienation suit at his office."

I hoped Al did not hear my little sigh of relief. I was afraid Alice might have written to him.

"Well, you'll just have to wait until you trace the gun," I said.

"No. I'm afraid even that won't help," he remarked regretfully.

"Why not?"

"Well, we ran into a little luck there," he explained. "We might have been busy for days tracing it if we hadn't. But I took a chance and sent wires to every city where I could connect with anybody who had anything to do with the case. I got a reply after I called you."

"Oh, Al! Tell me."

"The gun was sold at a pawn shop in El Paso about six years ago. That's the last sale on it we can find."

"Six years ago," I murmured. "El Paso? Al don't tell me it was Frank's own gun!"

"Exactly. Frank bought it in El Paso six years ago."

"But who—I mean—" I felt a little dazed, and Al patted my hand.

"Don't be so dumbfounded, Isabel," he directed. "He didn't commit suicide on those steps. But here *is* the point. We can't possibly tell, from that, who might have had the gun, because anybody might have had it. Suppose Frank bought it because he was moving around some pretty tough districts. All right; after he gets home he doesn't need it any more and he tosses it into a drawer and forgets he has it. When Mrs. Murdock goes to Reno she may see it and pack it, maybe thinking a gun would come in handy in the Wild West. That's just a possibility, you see; I'm not saying any of these is correct. But Mrs. Emory-Murdock might have had it with her, and Emory himself could easily have said it wasn't safe for her to have around. He'd carry it. Or Murdock kept it, and had it in his apartment, where James could have taken it any time he wanted it."

"Did you ask him that?" I interrupted.

"Yes. James denies ever having seen Frank with a gun, or any pistol in Frank's possession. He denies having it himself. But he'd lie about that, I imagine, if he *had* had it. And then let us try to prove it. And those aren't all the possibilities, even yet. The fair Doris had two ways of getting it, if she wanted it. Either from the Emories, if they had it, or from Frank himself. Suppose she told him, in Reno, that she was nervous in the rented house with only another woman and a young child. Frank might have lent it to her, and forgotten to get it back.

"And if there is the other woman everybody's harping about, she might have gotten it the same way."

I had already realized that. And I remembered suddenly that Alice Trent was an excellent shot. She had been skeet champion of our town in the East for two years, and I knew that she had been practicing with a pistol since the war started, with several other ambitious women. Both she and Burton were ardent hunters, and probably had an arsenal in the house. All the more reason, I thought, why they would use Frank's own gun, if they had access to it.

I realized suddenly in what direction my thoughts had been straying, and promptly frowned. All of that was ridiculous, of course. Burton wouldn't—As for Alice, she was not quite my idea of a wildly jealous woman. But if she *had* thought Frank and Doris—

I shook my head, while Al watched my little performance curiously.

"Think of something?" he asked.

"No." I had to make an excuse at once, and my mind seemed completely blank. "I was just wondering," I said lamely, "whether it doesn't all point back to James, after all. That seems most likely."

"It does," he admitted, "but we've got to have something more substantial than that to go on. I'm afraid, Isabel, we're up against it, unless we discover our Other Woman. Any ideas about it?"

"None," I declared firmly, and looked at him. His expression was grim, and not so friendly as usual.

"I wish I knew what goes on in your mind, Isabel. I think, if you did know, and knew her, you'd blow up before you'd tell me. In a murder case loyalties are sometimes out of place, you know."

I felt my cheeks turning pink in spite of myself.

"Al, I don't think I'd ever try to conceal anything from you that would really solve a case," I said evasively, but with great earnestness.

"But you'd be the judge, is that it?"

I did my best to look him directly in the eye. It wasn't so hard, at that, but I knew perfectly well he suspected me of withholding something.

"Yes, Al. I'd be the judge, I think," I told him. He shrugged.

"And that's all I'll get out of you. But, Isabel, if you make a mistake—"

"Then, Al, I'll run to you right away. I promise that."

With that he was content. But I was glad when he rose in a few moments to go. I found I was shaking all over.

## *Chapter* XIV

I HAD intended to go to Cora's alone, but on an impulse I telephoned Alice to discover whether or not she was invited, and to suggest that she go with me. She had almost decided not to go she told me over the phone. A slight headache, she explained. I told her I thought it would do her good, and that I would be around for her in ten minutes.

"All right," she said, "but if I snap somebody's head off before the afternoon's over, it won't be my fault."

I offered to share the responsibility, and hung up.

She was a little distrait when I reached the house, and still puzzling over whether to wear her chartreuse wool or the little black model with the blue jabot. While she was deciding, I sat on the edge of her bed wondering how to broach the subject I had in mind. Tact prevented me, very definitely, from being quite candid. I had to approach the subject warily.

It seemed to me very important to find out whether or not Burton had any hint of Alice's relationship with Frank. If he hadn't, we could both forget the matter at once. If he had, then, very certainly, something had to be done about it. I had no intention of defeating the ends of justice, which I more or less believed Al to suspect. I wanted only to save Alice every possible inconvenience and unhappiness, if I was convinced neither she nor Burton were involved.

My brother Web would have called that unwarranted meddling, but on the whole I did not look upon it quite that way.

I sat on the edge of Alice's bed, wondering how to open the subject. She was fingering her clothes in the closet, still undecided. She finally selected a dull red crepe, and pulled it off its hanger.

"I hope Cora doesn't notice anything odd about me," she said vaguely, taking the dress with her to her dressing-room. "Wait just a second, my dear, and I'll be right with you."

The moment she vanished, pulling the door shut behind her, I rose and went to the closet. If my conscience bothered me, I silenced it rudely.

Burton's suits—and he seemed to have dozens—were neatly hung on a rod, side by side. I glanced at them swiftly, one after the other, without finding anything. It was a negative result, but one that pleased me. Still, I realized it was far from a complete search. I was about to turn away from the closet when I saw a dark suit hung on a hook at the back. With one ear alert for sounds of Alice in the dressing-room, I pulled the trouser legs into sight, and inspected them. The cuffs were speckled with tiny spots of dried mud. Inside the cuff was the usual accumulation of dust, and something much more important. There were bits of weeds— things that looked like wild oat kernels, and half a dozen tiny green triangles that clung like leeches to the cloth. I have no idea what kind of weed they are, but I never walk through a vacant lot without coming out with my skirts covered with them.

I pried one loose with my fingernail, and looked at it. Just then I heard Alice moving in the dressing-room, and I dropped the trouser leg hastily, and backed out of the closet. When she came in I was sitting innocently on the bed inspecting my fingernails. The little burr was in my bag.

"I'll be with you in a moment," she said. "I want to remind Caroline to send Burton's suit out to be cleaned."

I could no more have prevented my guilty start than I could have swum the Pacific. But fortunately Alice was looking the other way, her finger on the bell to the kitchen.

"I don't know where Burton picked up all those prickly things on his trousers," she remarked. "I noticed them this afternoon, and you can't get them off. He was over at Mr. Wood's last night, and I can't imagine any place there where he'd get them. The Woods' garden is the envy of everybody in Holmby Hills."

"Wood?" I asked, as casually as I could. "I don't believe I know him."

"He's an engineer," she explained. "He and Burton have been working out ways of speeding up production, and Burton went over last night to get some blueprints from him. Awfully nice people, the Woods. I'll take you over there sometime, Isabel. You'd love their roses. Mrs. Wood is a fanatic about roses."

"I'd like to meet them," I said, trying to make my voice sound natural. I was convinced of one thing, at least; that Alice had no idea whatever that Burton suspected anything. Those burrs weren't proof of anything, either. You find them, as I knew, in almost any overgrown spot. But clearly Alice did not associate them with the Emories' heavily-weeded barranca. I decided not to bring up the subject at all just then.

We drove over to Cora's, a matter of only a few blocks, to find her patio filled to overflowing with a miscellany of guests. When Cora entertains, she keeps open house. I am always prepared to find the grocer clerk there too—Cora would be so apt to tell him she was buying the liverwurst for appetizers for cocktails, and why doesn't he drop in later? I have, of course, not ever faced that particular situation, but it wouldn't surprise me. And I always know that at least half the guests will be strangers to me, and, not infrequently, strangers to Cora as well.

It was some time before we found Cora, and we mingled, nodding or speaking to the people we knew, and eyeing the strangers with that tentative friendliness that is always so timid.

Alice stayed close beside me, as if she were deliberately avoiding people, breaking into animated conversation the moment anyone we knew seemed to be approaching, and lapsing once more into silence when they had drifted past.

"Cora's place looks lovely, doesn't it?" she bubbled, in one of these garrulous interludes. "I wonder if her gin is better than it used to be, or should we insist on highballs?"

"I stuck to Scotch yesterday," I replied.

"Yesterday? Were you here yesterday?"

"Yes. Cora gives her parties three or four days in succession. She can't crowd all her acquaintances in on one day."

"How odd. I never knew that. She is a dear, though, isn't she? Oh, look, there's Mr. Wood. Remember I mentioned him?"

She pointed to a stout baldish man who was talking to a thin, shriveled woman in white. He had a very red face, and a large expanse of vest showing.

"He doesn't look a bit like an engineer to me," I said.

"No. He doesn't, does he? But he's absolutely brilliant."

Cora came up then and became properly effusive in her greetings. Almost before we knew it we had Martinis in our hands, and were admiring her new tea gown.

"It's the very last I'm going to get for the Duration," said Cora. "Unless, of course, the Duration lasts too long and we're simply in rags. But I don't feel it's patriotic. And as for entertaining, I've just cut down to the bone. I limit myself to cocktail parties entirely now. No dinners, no luncheons, except for the Red Cross or something. And, Isabel, I'm going to open a canteen next week. In the cutest uniform. Of course I don't think that's like a new dress, do you? That's practical."

It seemed incredible to me that she had not read of the murder in the papers, and did not mention it, until it occurred to me that the duties of hostess made it an essential of tact to avoid such unpleasant subjects.

As usual at Cora's gatherings, I drifted away from Alice and Cora, eventually, and lost sight of them completely. But for once it was a deliberate maneuver on my part. I sidled—no other word quite conveys it—toward the rotund Mr. Wood, hovering in his vicinity until he spoke to someone I knew, and then approaching boldly, quite sure of an introduction. It came as I expected. I found myself shaking hands with Mr. Wood, my own small hand enveloped in genial heartiness to the point where I almost yelped.

"I understand you and Mr. Trent are doing work together," I said conversationally.

"Yes, indeed! Do you know Burt?"

"Oh, yes. I've known him for years. We come from the same New England town."

"Well, well, it's a small world, isn't it?" He beamed at me, as if I were a brand new discovery.

"It is indeed. Mrs. Trent was mentioning to me only this afternoon that Burt had been at your place yesterday evening," I said, with subtle intent. He smiled back.

"I must have them bring you sometime," he said. "Like roses?"

"I adore them. I hear your wife is a marvelous rose-grower."

"Indeed she is! I prefer the yellow things, myself—you know, nasturtiums, marigolds, all those orange things. Roses need too much spraying and pruning and fussing. But they look pretty."

"Well, I'd love to see them," I assured him. "Sometime when Burt isn't coming out to see you on business, as he did last night, I'll have him bring me."

"I would be honored, Miss Marsh," he declared, with a little bow that compressed his mid portions into a series of ample wrinkles. "Why don't all of you come tomorrow evening? I'll speak to Burt about it as soon as I see him."

"That would be splendid," I said. "If it's not too early in the evening."

But the fiendish perversity that throws wrenches into the subject plans of mice and men still persisted. After all, I couldn't very well ask him outright what time Burton Trent had arrived and left the night before. I had to bide my time.

I had almost given up completely when an opportunity came to learn what I wanted. I had lingered beside him longer than the casual introduction would warrant, talking almost as much at random as Alice had, before he finally returned to the subject.

"So you know Burt! Well, well! I have supper with him almost every night these days."

"Really?" I said, with much more interest than so simple a statement called for.

"Yes. We're both very busy men these days, and it's about the only chance we get to have a little conference. Both of us hate to bother our wives talking shop, so we eat at a good steak house somewhere, and thrash out plans."

"Don't your wives feel a little neglected?" I asked.

"I hope they do, God bless 'em!" said Mr. Wood, with a deep chuckle. "It's one of their patriotic duties, however."

I took my courage in hand, risking the chance that he would consider me a prying woman. Assuming almost an arch look, and feeling extremely silly, I asked, "Did you dine together last night? I thought Alice told me Burt went over to your house later in the evening."

If he thought the question impertinent, he had the courtesy to conceal it.

"Oh, that was because my assistant had drawn up some blueprints and I wanted to go over them with Burt before I handed them over. We had dinner at Henry's. Do you know the place? On La Cienega, and the steaks are delicious."

"No, I've never been there," I said. "I must try it."

"I can recommend it highly. I wanted Burt to come directly home with me from there, but he had an appointment somewhere for eight o'clock, so I went home and waited for him. He got there around nine. Don't think my wife and I didn't kid him!"

"Kid him? What about?"

"Oh, his appointment! He wouldn't tell us what it was, and I insisted he sneaked off to see an old flame." Mr. Wood laughed heartily. "Do you think he'd loosen up then and tell us? Not Burt! But you know him. He just smiled back. Great guy, Burt!"

I agreed that Burt was a great guy. He nodded, and noticed my empty glass.

"Let me get you a fresh drink, Miss Marsh," he offered.

"I—oh, thanks, don't bother!" I begged. "I have to run along anyway. And I'm looking forward to seeing those roses."

"You bet! I'll call Burt about it."

I escaped from him, and went to find Alice. I don't know how I looked, but several people turned to watch me curiously, and Alice gave an exclamation of alarm when she saw me.

"Isabel, what's wrong? You're white as a sheet."

"I'm perfectly all right," I protested. "But I could stand another Scotch. A stiff one."

<hr>

## Chapter XV

<hr>

I HAD no appetite when I got home that evening, what with the hors-d'oeuvres at Cora's and my own confused mental condition. I had something to figure out, and food seemed to be merely an unnecessary distraction. Fern was solicitous and pressed on me a tempting platter of lamb chops, but I merely picked at one while I wondered what to do about Burton Trent.

I was convinced, now, that I should tell Al what I had learned, and leave it to him to make what he could of it. I had no proof of anything, merely a strong suspicion. Burton had left Mr. Wood and then rejoined him; he had been somewhere during just the time when he *could* have been at the Emories', and he had been very reluctant, to put it mildly, to tell where he had been. He had had burrs on his trouser legs, as anyone would have who had wandered through the Emories' grounds. But, on the other hand, it was possible that he had had a legitimate appointment, far from the Emories', and for some reason simply didn't want to tell Mr. Wood. And even I knew that burrs can be picked up anywhere, in almost any vacant lot.

I doubted if I could find out any more for myself without starting people to wonder why I was becoming so curious. Certainly I couldn't go to Burton and ask him outright where he had been. And if I did lapse so far from normal courtesy, he would only have to tell me that he had had an appointment, to silence me completely.

And yet I still hesitated to say anything to Al. Proof *was* lacking, and I had nothing to show even a probability that it was Burton I had seen outside the Emory house. It had been far too dark to recognize anyone.

I decided to say nothing at all—yet.

But once back in my den, with a fire going, I could not even settle down to reading about Columbus. I merely sat and stared into the firelight, feeling lonely and very uneasy. I almost jumped out of my chair when the phone rang, suddenly and noisily, around eight-thirty.

I did not wait for Fern to answer it. I was anxious to talk to someone—anyone—and I reached for the receiver in relief.

At first I did not recognize the woman's voice at all. It was a low voice without character, speaking in a monotone that was a little muffled. It sounded as if someone were talking very quietly with her lips close to the transmitter.

"Is this Miss Marsh?" the voice asked.

"Yes. Who is speaking?"

"Are you alone, Miss Marsh?"

"Yes. But who are you?"

"You're quite sure no one is with you?" the voice asked, a trace of urgency sounding through the monotone.

"Quite. I can't understand, though, why—"

"Please! It's very important. I'm Doris Ayers."

"Oh, Miss Ayers!" I said, a little relieved. "Is Mrs. Emory all right?"

"Yes. She's all right. I'm not calling for her. I haven't much time. I'd rather they didn't know I had called you. But something's been troubling me."

"What is it?"

"I can't tell you over the phone. The house is full of extensions. But I want to ask your advice."

"Can't you give me an idea of what about?" I begged.

"Well, you know when—when it happened last night, I told you I was in the kitchen. I think I did correct that statement. Well, I was upstairs in my room for a moment. I'll explain it all later. I saw something—something very important. I've been trying to decide all day what to do. I haven't told the police, and I feel I should. But I'd like to ask you about it first."

"I'd advise you to tell them at once, whatever it is," I said a little shortly.

"You might not think so, if you knew. Please, won't you see me and let me explain?"

Her voice was still low, still without character, almost as if she were whispering.

"But where, Miss Ayers? Shall I come to the house?"

"No. No, that wouldn't do. And I can't leave long enough to come to your place. I know this is an imposition, but I'm sure if you let me talk to you you'll see that it's terribly important. Do you remember the street the house is on?"

"Yes," I replied.

"You know that just beyond the house it goes around a circle. There's grass there and a few trees. Elaine and I often play there in the afternoon. At night sometimes I see people sitting on the benches there. I'm sure I could meet you there without attracting attention. Can you meet me there at nine o'clock?"

"I suppose I could," I said slowly. "You're sure it's important?"

"I assure you it is."

"Very well. I'll try and be there."

"Thank you. I'll be at the north side of the circle."

She hung up then before I had a chance to say anything more.

I sat by the phone for a minute or two, thinking. It seemed an odd thing for Miss Ayers to do, when I considered it, though it was possible that she knew something, and had the feeling that it might clear things up. But why shouldn't she ask Joan's advice, rather than mine? Was it that she disliked Joan and, perhaps, distrusted her? Perhaps she thought that because I knew Captain Branson personally, I could pass her information along without involving her. But it was odd, nevertheless; and the time and place she had chosen made it more curious than ever.

But if she had hoped to bring me to the circle she could hardly have chosen a better method. I have an enlarged bump of curiosity. She had made the whole matter sound so mysterious I doubt whether I could have resisted the temptation to meet her and find out what it was she wanted.

I had half an hour until the time I was supposed to meet her. It would not take me more than ten minutes to drive to the circle, and I had no intention of arriving early and having to wait alone, and possibly conspicuously, if any cars passed, until she joined me. I waited twenty minutes, therefore, with as much patience as I could muster, and then went out to my car, parked on my driveway, and started toward Bel-Air.

The evening was cloudy and very damp. My windshield was completely fogged, and I had to wipe it off before I could even see to drive. The streets, too, seemed strangely lonely. There was a stream of cars moving along Sunset Boulevard, but not so many as there had been a few months before. And houses were not so brightly lighted. The war had seemed to infect us, making us conscious of the dark and its lurking dangers.

I was glad when I reached the street where the Emories lived, and turned in. It was darker than Sunset, however, shaded with thick old eucalyptus trees, and the street lights were far apart. Lights were burning in the Emories' when I passed the house, but it had, in spite of them, a dead look.

The circle was not far beyond—perhaps half a block, no more. It was, I suppose, about two hundred feet wide, mostly open lawn, with thick clusters of trees at the north and south arcs. There were flower beds there, and one or two benches. I saw, as I approached it, that there were no street lights near it. Such lights as there were, were across the street and almost buried in foliage. The whole circle was in deep shadow.

A belated sense of uneasiness began to plague me. I realized suddenly, as I parked my car just beyond the circle, that I was probably doing a very foolish thing. I should certainly have told Al where I was going. But if I had, I knew he would have forbidden it, and gone himself. Doris would probably have seen him coming and disappeared, or refused flatly to speak to him.

I locked the car, and started to cross the street to the north side of the circle. I felt a little frightened, and annoyed with myself for feeling that way. I refused to give in to my wiser instincts. Sheer curiosity, and stubbornness, I think, carried me across the street and into the thickness of the trees.

There was no other sound in the circle. I glanced at my watch, which was only a grey blur. Perhaps, I thought, I was a minute or two early, or Miss Ayers was late. I decided to find a bench, to sit there for ten minutes and no more, and then, if Miss Ayers had not come, to go home at once and telephone Al.

Somehow that decision made me feel a little better. I went on more boldly, pushing through the trees to the open circle where I knew the benches were. A car passed by on the street, but its headlights illuminated only the opposite side of the street as it swung around the circle, making the shadows seem all the heavier.

I reached one of the two benches and looked around. No one was in sight anywhere. I could make out the outlines of the other bench a little distance away, and nearer the trees. No one seemed to be near it, but I crossed toward it, and as I did I called Miss Ayers' name softly. There was no answer.

I sat down, and tried to listen for footsteps, but I could hear only a rhythmic throbbing that I suddenly realized was the beating of my heart. Very clearly I recalled the figure outside the Emories' window, a furtive, dark shape; and now the trees behind me seemed to me to be filled with dark shapes, sinister and deadly.

It was impossible to sit still. I was frightened, and no longer stubborn or even curious. I wanted to go home, and intended to go no matter what happened now.

I stood up and glanced around. The shadows were all around me, menacing. They had no shape—none but the dark shadow on the ground near the bench, which I had not seen until then, a shadow that was out of place, thrown by no tree or bench or flower bed.

It wasn't a shadow at all, I realized, but something dark and crouching by the trees. Something bulky and low, like a large dog lying in wait. I strained my eyes to see it better, and saw only a blur. When I glanced away a little I could make it out better. There were patches of white on it.

And then I knew, without looking, what it was. I was too terrified to scream; my throat was completely constricted. But in a moment I was down on my knees in the soaking grass, feeling the limp body.

It was Doris. I recognized her even in the darkness, the round, stolid face, her eyes staring sightlessly, her skin a horrible color. She was wearing the dark blue dress I had seen her in before, only the small organdy collar making a spot of white. I had been within ten feet of her and had not seen her. Her dress was too dark.

I got to my feet somehow. I could think only of escape, of fleeing from that inhuman dead thing, and the power that had struck her down, still lingering, perhaps, in the shadow of the trees. For her body was still warm.

## Chapter XVI

I⁢T WAS only a few steps to the Emories' house, but I could have been stumbling across the Matto Grosso, it seemed to take so long for me to cross that dark street and thread my way through the pepper trees and shrubbery to their front door. When

I found the bell, hidden in a mass of ivy, I put my finger on it and held it there.

I didn't know who was in the house, and I didn't very much care. I wanted to be indoors, with lights burning and people around me, and the sooner the better. Once I had achieved that, I could take time to figure out what to do next.

Sarah Bentley came hurrying through the hall, drawing open the peephole in the door to stare out at me. It's a wonder she opened the door at all, because I must have looked like an ashen Medusa. But she threw open the door and put her arm around my shoulders and led me in.

Al and Thorne were standing in the hallway, regarding me with mingled curiosity and alarm. I shook off Sarah's protecting arm and flung myself on Al, all maidenly restraint forgotten.

"Oh, Al," I sobbed, "it's so horrible out there for her, all alone. Go to her! Please, somebody go to her!"

He patted me gently until I could control myself, sensibly asking no questions as the average well-meaning male would have done. I think Thorne was too surprised to do anything but stare at me.

"Now," Al said finally, "what's the big fuss, Isabel?"

"It's Doris Ayers. She's outside there, dead."

"Dead? How—?"

"I don't know. I just found her lying by the bench at the circle. She looked awful. All purple and—"

I started shaking, then, and he half carried me into the living-room, to the sofa. Sarah hovered solicitously beside me, and at Al's sharp order, scurried away for brandy. Thorne still stood, like an unpleasant cherub, eyeing me in unfriendly fashion. I did not even see Al leave the room, and it was some minutes after the brandy had arrived, and Thorne had sat down opposite me to ask questions, before he returned. He shooed Thorne out at once.

"I'll talk to her, Emory," he said firmly. "Too many of us will upset her. She's had a bad shock. I'd appreciate it if you'd wait in the library."

Thorne was not used to being ordered around, especially in his own house, but he took it with good grace, asked if there was anything he could do, and drifted out. I heard Joan's voice just then, calling him from upstairs, and he went up to stay with her.

Al waited until my color was a little more normal, rubbing my hands meanwhile.

"I don't suppose you feel like telling me what happened, do you?" he asked. "I'd like to know."

"I just found her lying there. Al, did you see her? Did you leave her lying out there all alone?"

"Hush, now. Don't think about that part of it. I ran up to the corner. There's an Air Raid Warden's house there, and the officer on local duty happened to be there. He's waiting by the body until the squad car gets here. Now, how on earth did you find her? She was completely hidden from the street."

"I went to meet her there."

"You went to meet her there!" he repeated incredulously. "Tell me about it."

I told him disjointedly but completely, beginning with the phone call and ending with my flight across the street. He listened absorbedly, shaking his head all the while as if he refused to believe it.

"Isabel!" he exclaimed, when I had finished, "how many times must I tell you— You'll get yourself murdered yet. Why didn't you try to get in touch with me first?"

"I don't know. I didn't dream there was any danger. It was almost across the street from the house . . ."

"And dark and lonely, with a murderer loose. Hereafter, if you ever get mixed up in anything like this again, I'm going to lock you up in the nearest cell where I can watch you until it's over."

"But, Al, what happened to her? Can you tell?"

He frowned at the carpet, his jaw very stern and immovable.

"She was strangled, Isabel. Just before you got there. I don't want to frighten you, but it seems to be the only way I can wake you up. The murderer was probably still among the trees there."

"How did he know I was going to meet her?"

"I don't know. Unless it was someone in this house, and they overheard her phone call. Did you hear any sounds over the phone that might have been someone listening in on an extension?"

"No. You usually can tell. But I don't remember anything like that. And who, in this house—?"

"I don't know," he repeated. "Mrs. Emory is still confined to bed, and I've been with Emory almost every second since he's been home. I brought him back here about half past eight."

"I wondered why you were here."

"That's why. We came in at half past eight, as I said."

"Doris called me just before that," I told him. "I looked at my clock when the phone rang, and again afterwards. He couldn't have listened in."

He shook his head slowly.

"He couldn't have, Isabel, if the call came before eight-thirty. He was with me until then. As soon as we got here he went upstairs to see his wife. He was up there about ten minutes; then he came down again. He might have overheard the conversation then, but that was about twenty minutes to nine. He was with me the rest of the time, in the living-room. A lot depends, of course, on when Doris Ayers went out. We'll have to find out."

He got up from the chair he had been sitting in, and rang the bell. Sarah came in promptly, looking frightened and on the verge of tears.

"I want to ask you a few questions," he said, in a friendly voice. "Your name is Sarah, isn't it?"

"Yes, sir."

"You know that Miss Ayers has had an accident, don't you?" Sarah's eyes were wide with horror.

"Yes, sir. I understood that. What—what happened?"

"We're afraid she was killed, just as Mr. Murdock was. Sarah, did you see her go out this evening?"

"Yes, sir. I did," she answered.

"Did you notice what time it was?" he asked.

Sarah shook her head. "I didn't notice the clock, sir. It was just a short time ago."

"I see. Well, think hard and see if you can time it—you know, tie it up with something to give an idea when it was."

"Well, sir, it was only a few minutes ago. You and Mr. Emory had come in—let me see, when Mr. Emory came down from Mrs. Emory's room he rang for me to bring in drinks."

"I remember that."

"Well, sir, it was when I was going back into the kitchen after I'd carried them to you. I saw her coming down the back steps, and she let herself out the back door."

"Did you talk to her?"

"No, sir. She'd gone out by the time I got into the kitchen. She seemed to be in a hurry, and trying to slip out without being seen. I thought it was kind of funny, because she can come or go as much as she pleases. But I guess, wherever she was going, she didn't want Mr. Emory to know about it."

"Was she wearing a hat or coat?"

"Oh, no, she didn't have a hat or a coat on. That's why I didn't think much about it then, except to think it was funny. I was sure she wasn't going far."

"I see. Thank you, Sarah. That's all right now."

Sarah bobbed her head, and returned to the kitchen. Al was silent a minute, thinking.

"I make that about ten to fifteen minutes of nine," he said finally. "We got here at eight-thirty, almost on the dot. Emory was upstairs about ten or twelve minutes—say twelve. It took about three or four minutes for Sarah to bring the drinks in. That's sixteen minutes, or in other words, fourteen minutes to nine that Doris went out. She must have crossed the street immediately, and found the murderer waiting for her."

"But I can't understand how the murderer knew—" I protested.

"It's just possible, Isabel, that she may have talked to him herself."

"I don't understand," I said. "I suppose I'm stupid, but I don't see."

"She called you at eight-thirty. She said she'd been wondering what to do, didn't she?" When I nodded, he continued, "In other words, whatever she wanted to tell you wasn't something she'd just discovered. She'd had time to think about it. Now, just suppose she'd seen something last night that struck her as odd. She'd wondered about it, without knowing exactly what it meant. She wanted to talk it over with somebody.

"Sometime today she may have talked to the murderer, not knowing at the time that he had shot Frank Murdock. She asked his advice, still not realizing the full significance of what she'd seen. He would of course, have told her to forget it, and she might, quite innocently, have said, no, she'd prefer to ask somebody else. She'd try and get you to meet her at the circle tonight.

"The murderer, then, had to stop her, for fear that when she told you, you'd tell me, and we'd realize how important the information was."

"I see. It's possible, of course. In fact, I can't imagine what else it could have been. But can't you discover, somehow, who she saw or spoke to today?"

There was an interruption, then. Sarah stood in the doorway, with the chauffeur beside her. He was not in uniform now. He was wearing a brown flannel suit, and looked very handsome, a tall, husky Irishman with blond hair and an open, friendly face.

"Pardon me, sir," Sarah said diffidently. "This is O'Hara, the chauffeur. We've been talking about poor Miss Ayers, and he's got something to tell you."

"Yes, O'Hara?" Al asked. "What is it?"

"About Miss Ayers, sir. You were asking about when she went out. I saw her."

"When and where, O'Hara? Come in and sit down."

He came further into the room, but he did not avail himself of Al's invitation to sit down. He remained standing, with Sarah behind him, her arms folded, and her eyes on him, almost like a proud mother watching her young son reciting a poem for company.

"My wife is cook here, you know, sir," he explained. "We have rooms over the garage. I was over there, after I'd helped in the kitchen to clear up the supper things. We'd gone over earlier than usual because Mr. Emory was out and Mrs. Emory just had a tray in her room.

"I was looking out of the window. I'd heard the kitchen door open—my window was up, it being stuffy in the room, sir—and I thought maybe Sarah might be wanting one of us for something and I looked out.

"But it was Miss Ayers. She came out and started to go down the drive. I was starting to come away from the window when I saw a man step out from the shade of one of those pepper trees. He went over and talked to her, and she looked up at our window, and then she kind of pulled him away down the drive, as if she didn't want to be seen. I couldn't see where they went. It was too dark to follow them that far from where I was."

Al had listened without putting in any questions. Now he asked, "Did you recognize the man?"

"No, sir. It was too dark to see anything except that it was a man."

"But you recognized Miss Ayers," Al pointed out.

O'Hara was apparently not confused.

"There wasn't much chance of mistaking her dark hair or her dress, sir. I saw those easy enough, and when she met the man she was further down the drive where it was much darker, with no light from the kitchen door to help."

"I see. You can't describe this man at all?"

"No, sir. Average size, he was, as far as I could see. Dark suit. I think he had a grey hat on, but I couldn't be sure of that, even."

That was all he could tell us, though Al continued to question him for several minutes.

"That's all, O'Hara," he said at last. "Thanks." He turned to me when the servants had gone. "What do you think now, Isabel? It sounds like your prowler again, doesn't it?"

"Yes," I admitted. I wondered how I could get away from Al long enough to use the phone. I felt, now, that I had to talk to Alice right away.

---

## Chapter XVII

---

THEN the police were there, and there was the familiar confused routine, the photographers, the police surgeon—all of it—while Thorne and I sat in the library, and Al directed the proceedings. Thorne did not talk much. His experience at Police Headquarters, I imagine, had subdued him. He looked very tired.

"This is getting pretty ghastly, Isabel," he said once. "Why don't they do something instead of fooling around?"

"Thorne," I asked, "do you know who did this? Have you any idea?"

"No, Isabel. Do you think I'd hide it if I knew? My God, if I'd known I might have saved Miss Ayers. It's awful to think about that."

"But, Thorne, who *could* have done it?"

He looked at me searchingly a moment.

"The only thing I can think of is some jealous woman, or her husband or lover. We all know what Frank was like."

"And have you anyone in mind?" I tried hard not to let him notice the eagerness in my voice.

"No," he said flatly. "Do you think I'd protect anyone if I thought he or she had committed murder?"

I didn't know. I could only shake my head.

"You don't know what Doris was trying to tell you?" he asked.

"No. She wouldn't tell me over the phone. I think she was afraid Joan or somebody might be listening."

"But why shouldn't Joan hear it? Why didn't she tell Joan instead of going to you?"

I could think of an answer to that, but it seemed more tactful not to mention it.

"Perehaps," I suggested instead, "she didn't want to worry Joan. The shock already has been hard on her. And you weren't here. She probably didn't know you were coming home."

"That's probably it," he admitted. "But if she'd only told you what it was. She didn't give you even a hint?"

"No."

"I'll have to find out what Doris did all day: where she went, if she was out; who she talked to on the phone," he said wearily. "Somewhere today she must have learned something. If we could only find out what it was."

"I know, Thorne. Would you mind very much if I used a phone? It's rather important. I—I want to tell Fern I won't be home for a while. She might worry."

"Oh, of course. Why don't you use the one in here?"

"Thanks."

I couldn't very well refuse, but that wasn't at all what I wanted. Surprisingly, Thorne suddenly showed consideration.

"I'm going up to sit with Joan," he said suddenly, rising. "If Captain Branson wants me, tell him I'm there. And help yourself to the phone."

I thanked him again, and waited until he had started up the stairs. Hastily I dialled Alice's number. She answered in a moment, a little surprised, I think, at my hurried, hushed voice.

"Alice, this is Isabel."

"Yes. I recognized you. Is anything wrong?"

"I'm afraid so. I'm at Joan's. The most awful thing has just happened. Doris Ayers has been murdered."

I had to hold the phone away from my ear for a while, her astonished voice became so piercing.

"Oh, how—how *awful!* Do they know who—?"

"No. They have no idea. I thought you'd want to know."

"Of course! I'm so glad you called. I'll tell Burton, too. He'll be so distressed!"

"Is he at home?"

"Yes. Yes, he's at home this evening."

I sighed with relief.

"Well, I'll see you tomorrow, Alice. I'll tell you about it then."

She thanked me again, and I hung the phone back on its stand. As I turned, I saw Al standing quietly in the doorway.

I had no idea how long he had been there. I must have looked like a guilty child caught stealing cookies, and I felt it. Al looked so very much like a stern parent.

"Whom were you talking to?" he asked, in that very firm tone which permits no evasion. "I want to know, Isabel."

"A friend of mine," I said feebly. "Oh, Al, it's not what you're thinking."

"Isabel, I'm very fond of you, and I wouldn't hurt you for the world. But I've got a job to do, and it's the kind of job that can't be interefered with. You've known something almost from the start that you haven't told me. I have to know what it is."

"It's nothing; I swear it, Al. I had a brainstorm this morning. I thought I saw something that wasn't there, that's all. Believe me."

"You were checking up just now to find out if somebody was at home, weren't you?"

"Yes, I was," I admitted. "He was. And that was all there was to that."

"Whoever he was, did you talk to him?"

"No, but Alice—" I bit my lip. "All right. His wife said he was at home."

"You had just told her there had been a murder, Isabel. If she had any reason to believe her husband was involved, she'd tell you exactly that. You've warned her, and given both of them a chance to cook up a story. Don't you realize you're putting yourself in the position of accessory?"

"Al," I pleaded, "don't look at me that way. I promised I wouldn't hide anything from you, if I had the least idea it was important."

"I believed you," he said, and sat down on the small leather sofa. "Now I think it's important, and I want you to tell me. Who is Alice, and what has her husband got to do with it? Remember that if you don't tell me, I have other ways of finding out, and they might not be so pleasant for your friend Alice."

There was nothing to do but tell him. In a way, it was a relief. The problem was too big for me to handle alone. And if Burton had been home, he and Alice had nothing to worry about.

"It was Alice Trent," I told him. "She knew Frank, Al. I haven't the slightest proof of it, but I think she was in love with him."

I told him the whole thing, then. About the burrs in the trouser cuffs, about Mr. Wood and the mysterious appointments. I even showed him the little green burr that I had put into my bag. He listened without commenting, until I had finished.

"I see," he said finally. "Well, if he was at home tonight, he has nothing to worry about. Or if he can tell us where he was last night before he arrived at Mr. Wood's."

"But if you do any questioning there, Al, please be careful," I begged. "If I've been all wrong, and Burton Trent had nothing whatever to do with it, he may not even know that Alice— You understand it would be hell for her if he found out."

"I understand perfectly." He looked down at the little green patch in his hand. "But I want an explanation of this, Isabel. That lower garden is all overgrown and full of these things."

"That's what I was afraid of."

He got up and began pacing slowly back and forth.

"Don't you see what a problem we're faced with?" he said pleadingly. "All we have learned so far is confused and inconclusive. A vague figure outside a door. A gun anyone might have had. Another vague figure outside the house tonight. It could have been anybody. We may have to uncover Frank Murdock's life for the past twenty years before we learn what we want.

"Perhaps your Burton Trent knows some of the answers. Perhaps he doesn't know anything at all. In that case where do we turn next? Is it someone we know about already, or some person we've never even heard about? Anybody at all can fire a shot through an open door. And anybody who ever knew Frank might have got hold of his gun.

"Well," he finished, "I'll tackle Burton Trent tomorrow—no, tonight, I think, if I clear things up here."

"Were there any signs—any clues out there?" I asked.

"No. Nothing. She was strangled, just a few minutes before you got there. The grass was moist, but there were no footprints that we could see—not even yours or hers. She was just lying there, dead. Isabel, did you see anything—anything at all out there that would help us? A car driving off. Even a parked car?"

I shook my head.

"The place was deserted. I remember that a car passed once, but it didn't stop. It went on up the street. But if somebody was still there, he could have hidden from me in those trees, and got away after I ran over here. If there was a car, it could have been parked in one of those streets that lead east from the circle. There are two, I think. Winding, residential streets, very dark."

"But you didn't see anything?"

"No."

"Well, we don't progress, then," he murmured. "I want to talk to Mrs. Emory. I don't care what Emory says. This is going too far. She may know something that would help. Someone in the past. I don't even know what. But I have to talk to her."

"I'll go up and tell her," I offered. "She'll let me in, and I think I can persuade her."

---

## Chapter XVIII

JOAN was sitting up in bed when I reached her room, looking frail and pallid in a pale green negligee. Thorne had been talking earnestly to her, but he stopped abruptly and rose.

"Come in, Isabel," he said superfluously.

"Thanks," I said, and sank down on the dressing-table chair.

"Isn't this whole thing shocking, Isabel?" Joan exclaimed, without any indication of grief. "And Miss Ayers, too! Thorne tells me she was trying to tell you something."

"Yes. But she never got the chance, poor soul."

"Oh, but that's impossible, Isabel! She *must* have told you something."

"I assure you she didn't, Joan."

"Her whole conduct was absurd," Joan declared acidly. "I can't understand why she'd turn to you that way. If she'd wanted anything, I was right here."

There was no point in being antagonistic, I realized, and I answered in a more friendly tone.

"It did seem rather disloyal. I'm sure she didn't want to worry you, that's all."

"Fiddlesticks! She never had that much consideration! Well, she's just managed to stir things up again."

"Yes. I'm sure she regrets it now," I couldn't help saying. "For heaven's sake, Joan! She's dead! If she was foolish, she paid for it with her life. Haven't you any feelings at all?"

"I don't pretend to have cared a great deal for Doris," she said. "Of course I'm shocked, and very sorry for her. But after all, it was her own fault."

I shrugged and delivered my message.

"Captain Branson wants to talk to you," I said. "Do you think you feel up to seeing him?"

"No, Joan doesn't," Thorne answered immediately.

"I still think I'd see him, Joan," I said, ignoring Thorne. "You're certainly not making a good impression."

That seemed to dawn upon her.

"What do you think, Thorne? Isabel may be right. And if you're in the room—"

"I advise against it," Thorne said without hesitation. "There's nothing you could tell him I can't tell him for you."

"Still—" she said thoughtfully.

I waited for her to make up her mind, glancing around the immaculate room meanwhile. It was immaculate, that is, except for a little dab of damp mud just inside the door, and I wondered whether it had been Thorne or myself who had tracked it in. I looked guiltily at my shoes. They were damp, but they were unstained by mud. Thorne's, then, I thought. He was wearing black shoes with spats. As I watched him he seemed almost to be conscious of my eyes on him, because he uncrossed his legs, and recrossed them. The soles of both his shoes were spotless.

It was a trifling thing, but it stayed in my mind, bothering me. I had an impulse to reach over and pick up the mud and drop it in the wastebasket, to restore the tidiness of the room.

"Isabel," Joan said sharply, "are you dreaming? I've spoken to you twice."

"What? Oh, I beg your pardon," I apologized, coming promptly out of my abstraction. "I was thinking. What did you say, Joan?"

"Tell Captain Branson I'll see him for five minutes," she said, graciously.

I got up.

"I'm glad you've decided that, Joan," I said. "Believe me, Captain Branson only wants to get this business straightened out."

"That's all right, Isabel," Thorne said. "I talked to him today. He understands our position. He won't annoy us."

I went downstairs, too angry with both of them to reply. Al was waiting in the library door, and joined me when I beckoned to him.

"Her Highness will grant an audience," I told him. "Limited to five minutes. The Prince Consort will remain in attendance and eject you forcibly, by the clock. Al, that woman is a heartless little b—"

"Isabel! Your language!" Al cautioned me, with a sudden grin. "If you were going to call her what I think you were."

"I don't care! She is, and I hope you scare the negligee off her."

Joan held out a limp hand to him as we entered. Her eyes were hollow, and the corners of her mouth drawn down. She looked incomparably more haggard than when I had left her a minute before. Well, I doubted whether Al would be taken in by that little play-acting.

"I won't keep you long, Mrs. Emory," he promised. "There are only one or two questions I want to ask you."

"I'm sure all of this is perfectly unnecessary," she said. "My husband could have told you everything."

"I'm interested first of all," he went on placidly, "in what Miss Ayers did today. Do you know?"

"Miss Ayers? I think she performed her duties until this evening."

"What were they?"

"Well, she had breakfast with Elaine, and then took her up the Glen to the riding academy there. She rides three times a week, you know. They came back for lunch, and then had a few lessons in the upstairs sitting-room. About three o'clock they went for a walk through Bel-Air. They got back at five, and I heard them playing badminton in the yard until Elaine's supper time at six. After that Miss Ayers read to Elaine, and I thought she was still with her when I heard what had happened."

"Where is your daughter now?"

"Asleep in her room. You don't want to disturb her, do you?"

Al was apologetic but firm.

"It's necessary, Mrs. Emory, to find out whether Miss Ayers had an opportunity to speak to anyone today. You tell me there were at least two times when that was possible. So, naturally, I must find out whether your daughter saw her talking to anyone."

It was a reasonable request, but they argued about it for a long time, and Al finally had to be content to wait until morning. He took his defeat with apparent resignation. In other things that he asked her, Joan was not helpful. She had been in her room, she said, when Frank was shot, and had seen nothing. As for Frank's past, he had lived apart from her so much that he might have met hundreds of people who might have had a reason for killing him. She knew of no one.

At the end of ten minutes Thorne rose and indicated very

plainly that the interview was over. Al expressed his regret at having had to disturb her and signalled to me to come along with him. We went down the steps slowly. As soon as I was out of earshot of the Emories I clutched his arm.

"Did you see it, Al?" I asked in a low voice.

"See what?"

"The mud on the floor?"

"Yes. Emory probably tracked it in."

"No. He didn't. His shoes were perfectly clean. But there was a pair of Joan's shoes kicked under the bed. The soles were caked with mud. I saw them plainly from where I sat."

---

## Chapter XIX

"JOAN has been out of her room some time this evening," I said firmly. "She's been out where it's muddy, Al. There's not a doubt of it."

"It looks that way," he said thoughtfully.

"What does that mean?"

"It could mean a lot of things, Isabel, and some of them perfectly innocent. Such as that she got tired of being in bed, and this evening, when nobody was around, she got dressed and went out into the garden for a walk. If the lawn had been watered, there'd have been mud on the paths somewhere, surely. And in a cool room like hers the mud might not dry hard for hours."

I was skeptical of that explanation, however.

"Joan has her faults," I said, "but she has a typical New England streak of tidiness. I can't quite see her kicking her shoes under the bed and leaving them there, muddy. If she really went out, she hung up the dress, didn't she? Why didn't she put the shoes in the closet too?"

"She didn't, though."

"Yes, and I'll bet it's because she was in a hurry. She had to get back to bed before someone found her. She had time, maybe, to hang up the dress, but someone came in before she could put her shoes away."

I don't know how impressed Al was with that idea, but he did not attempt to refute it.

"In any case, Isabel, it doesn't necessarily mean that she went out to the circle, if that's what you're hinting at. You were out there. Your own shoes are damp and a little grass-stained. But there's no mud on them."

I refused to let Al drive home with me, though I did let him walk to my car with me, where it was parked further up the street.

"You'll promise to go straight home?" he asked, as I put the key in the ignition. "And lock your doors and windows tight tonight?"

"I promise."

"When the whole business is over, Isabel, I—"

"Please, Al. Not tonight, I'm worn out."

"I was just going to say, I'll feel a lot easier in my mind about you. You know you *might* know something, just the way Doris Ayers did, that our murderer wouldn't want you to know."

"Oh! Well, everything I know you know too, now. And if there's anything in any of it to incriminate anybody, certainly I can't see it. Suspicions—yes, dozens. But proof? Where is it, Al?"

"In time, my dear. And now you stay at home until I call you tomorrow."

I was not molested that night either, but I did not know until long afterward that Al had had a man guarding my house all night. He wasn't taking any chances.

For some reason, too, he failed to make his promised visit to the Trents'. that night. As he said afterwards, my phone call had already done the damage, and warned them. They might well have had a story prepared by the time he got there; and it did no great harm to allow them to sleep on it. He was certain Burton would make no attempt to run away, and to make sure of that he posted a man at their house too.

Early the following morning he telephoned me.

"Just wanted to know if you were all right," he explained. "I think I'll keep you under my eye today, Isabel, if you don't mind. I'm not sure I trust your own sleuthing impulses. You might get in trouble."

"If that's all you think of the help I've given you," I protested.

"That's how much I think of it. Lunch at some place on the Strip?"

He knew how to tempt me.

"It's a date," I agreed. "But, Al, promise me. No more shudders and horrors. This case has had me torn apart like a worn handkerchief."

"I promise. Strictly routine today."

He stopped by for me at nine, looking very fresh and dapper. It was a cloudy day, however, and my spirits were low and picked up only slightly when I saw him.

"I think we may make some progress today," he said. "I could let Green or one of the other detectives do most of this, but, frankly, Isabel, there's so little to work on except this that I feel better handling it myself."

I asked him what he meant by "this."

"Alibis," he said, as he turned his car toward Sunset Boulevard. "And now we have to get a double set from everybody—one for Thursday night, one for last night."

"I always did think that movie business of James' the other night sounded fishy. Did you find out where he was last night? He could easily have been the man Doris went out with."

"I've had a man watching him ever since I first saw him. I have a full account of what he did all day yesterday. He slept late, then called the police to find out what he could do about funeral arrangements. We told him he'd have to wait until after the inquest, which is set for Monday. I dropped in during the morning to question him again, and after I left he wrote letters in his apartment, went to market before lunch, and prepared his meal in his rooms. During the afternoon he shopped in Beverly Hills. I don't think he really wanted to buy anything; he was just trying to keep busy. He didn't see anybody or talk to anybody but the salespeople. He made one telephone call in the afternoon. We can't trace it, unfortunately. It was a dialled number."

"Doris?" I asked.

"I thought so, at first. But he made the call at about the time that Mrs. Emory says Doris was out with Elaine. So I'm pretty sure he didn't talk to her. He had an early supper at a restaurant on Wilshire Boulevard, and went to the movies—a theater on Wilshire—about seven-thirty."

"There goes another theater alibi. Al, are you sure—?"

"Wait. My man followed him in. It was dark in there after coming in from the street, which was still light at that time—War Time, you know. So my man missed him, and couldn't spot him in the theater. Instead, he came out and parked the car he'd been

using, in front of the theater, and waited. James came out at ten-
ten, at the end of the double feature, went home, and stayed there.
We don't know he stayed in the theater the whole time, I admit.
But if he didn't, I don't see how he got back in again without
buying another ticket, and my man swears he didn't do that.
There was a strong light on the ticket booth, and my man wasn't
a dozen feet away.

"But on Thursday night I'm not so sure he did stay in the
theater."

He had turned up Sunset, past the Beverly Hills Hotel, and he
drew the car up there and parked near the little shed which
was the bus station.

"What are we stopping here for?" I asked.

"You'll see in a minute or two," he replied, looking at his watch.
"Let me finish telling you about James. Thursday, of course, he
had no one following him. I doubt if anyone would be apt to notice
whether he went in or out of the theater. Certainly no one did
notice. We checked that yesterday. We know his car was parked
near the theater, but there are other ways of traveling."

"By bus!" I said, seeing daylight at last.

"Yes." Al nodded approvingly. "Now here's a little time-table
I made out, and I think it's rather significant. James left his
apartment at seven-fifteen to go to the movie theater. It wasn't
far, but he might have had to look around for a space to park.
And if he wanted an alibi, he would deliberately look for a place
where he'd be pretty sure to get a ticket. Say that took ten minutes. At seven-thirty, or about that, he bought a ticket and went
into the theater.

"Now, according to the time-table of the Pacific-Electric coach
lines, a bus heading toward Bel-Air passed one block from that
theater at seven-forty. It reached Bel-Air at eight-three. From the
corner it wouldn't be five minutes' walk to the Emories'. It was
around eight-thirty when you saw the man out in the yard."

"About that," I confirmed.

"Good. Then the shot was fired about eight-forty. At eight-
fifty-four that same bus reached Bel-Air heading back to Los
Angeles. It got to the corner near the movie theater, according to
the schedule, at nine-fifteen. The double feature would be over at
ten-thirty, and James arrived home at ten-forty-five. How does
that strike you?"

"Al, it's almost too perfect to be true."

"That," he admitted, "is the only thing that bothers me. If James had prepared an alibi, wouldn't he have known we'd check?"

"I suppose he would. And that's what you're doing now?"

"Yes. The driver of that bus is to meet me here at nine-thirty-eight. It's nine-thirty now."

We sat talking in the car until the large red bus pulled up at the station, and disgorged a passenger or two. One of them was a bus driver who looked up and down the street after he had alighted, and approached us when he saw Al's signal.

"I'm Captain Branson," Al said. "You're Martindale?"

"Yes," the bus driver said, and shook hands.

"Get in the car, Martindale. We can talk in here. I may want to drive you downtown to identify someone, if you can."

"O.K.," said the driver, and climbed into the back seat. Al and I swiveled around on the front seat to face him.

"I'm trying to trace the movements of a man who may have taken your bus last night—the seven-twenty from Pershing Square," Al explained. "I want your help."

"Yes, sir." Martindale waited eagerly.

"Do you remember a man who got on at—" Al named the corner—"and rode to Bel-Air on that bus?"

Martindale smiled a little.

"No, I do not," he said with conviction. "That run is usually an empty one westward anyway. Wrong hour. All the way to the Palisades there aren't many people aboard. Coming back on the eastward run I'm usually crowded when I'm driving that particular bus. Maids, mostly, coming home at night.

"But I can tell you this. There wasn't a man that got on where you said and went to Bel-Air. I know that for a fact. From the Beverly Hills Hotel here until I got past Bel-Air, I had three passengers, all of them women. I picked up a man at Veteran, but that's beyond where you're interested in, I guess."

"I guess it is," Al admitted, in a disappointed voice. "You're quite sure of that, Martindale?"

"Quite sure."

"You're not confusing it with some other trip?"

"No, sir. I was working early shift yesterday, and that was the last night run I've made. I remember it pretty well. I remember even the return load wasn't as big as usual. Thursday's maid's day off, you know."

"Did you, by any chance, pick up a man at Bel-Air and take him in to the other corner on the return trip?"

"No, sir. There was a colored maid from Bel-Air. I know her; I've been carrying her for about two years. No one else."

"All right, then. If a person somewhere near Beverly Boulevard and La Brea around seven-thirty wanted to get to Bel-Air by eight-twenty, is there any other way he could go?"

"Not by bus," Martindale said promptly. "There's other buses and ways of transferring, of course. But I know the schedules well enough to know my bus was the only one that would fill in that hour." He was emphatic about it, and Al finally let him go. He and I sat in the car a moment, thinking.

"Taxi," I said finally.

"Too risky," Al said at once. "A bus driver might not notice one man, and James might have taken a chance. But a cab to Bel-Air is expensive, and the driver would remember."

"Let me think. Bicycle?" I remembered the Dodge case, where a bicycle had solved a tricky transportation problem.

"Too long a ride for that. No," said Al. "That's out, too."

"Well," I suggested, "how about his own car? He got his ticket at eight-twenty, didn't he? What was to prevent him from getting back in it right after that, and driving out? He could make it, couldn't he?"

"Not in ten minutes. No. I don't think so. It takes the bus twenty-three minutes. At best it would take him fifteen. But in any case he couldn't do it. I've talked to the officer who gave him the ticket, and he saw the car still there at eight-forty."

"It almost looks as if we're on the wrong track," I said.

"It does. Unless the taxi idea works out, and I don't count on that. What do you say we cross off friend James for the time being, anyway, and pay a little visit to Burton Trent?"

## Chapter XX

As we drove toward Alice Trent's, I began to have a sinking feeling—that uncomfortable sensation you get when the dentist's nurse pokes her head into the waiting room and says, "Next!" to you. Whatever happened when we reached there,

I felt sure Burton's and Alice's lives would never be quite the same afterwards. I wanted, suddenly, not to be there when Al talked to them, and I told him so, very firmly.

"You don't have to be, if you'd rather not," he said. "Just sit in the car."

"I'd rather, Al. It seems so cold-blooded, a friend going in there. They may have to drag a few skeletons out of the closet, and it's all right for you to do the dragging, because you're official, and confidential if you can be. But in front of me—Alice would never face me again."

"I see your point. All right. You stay in the car."

"Al," I said, as he swung into a palm-lined street, "I may be all wrong about Burton, you know, and those burr things on his trousers. He could get them so many places. It doesn't really mean anything. How do you know James' trousers weren't covered with them too?"

"Do you think we didn't look?" he asked. "We examined every suit he owned including one at the cleaner's. No burrs."

"And yet, if he'd had them, he might have picked them off. You can do it, you know. It's not like blood stains or anything like that."

"That's true enough. If your friend Trent can give me a good explanation of where he got the burrs on his own trousers, I'll be glad to hear it."

To my dismay, Alice was in her front yard when Al parked at the curb. She was picking the young petunias, and spotted me right away, coming over at once to say hello. I had to introduce Al to her.

"This is Captain Branson, Alice. Of the Sheriff's Office."

"Oh," she said, and her face, for a moment, looked drawn. "How do you do."

"I dropped by to ask you a few questions," Al said in a manner that was not unfriendly, but not cordial either.

"About—about Frank Murdock?" she asked.

"Yes. May I come in?"

"Of course," she replied, but her voice was dull. "Did Isabel— Miss Marsh tell you to come?"

"Alice," I said earnestly, "I've done everything in my power to keep him away. Believe me, my dear."

"I suppose you did. It wasn't much use, was it? Captain Branson, please come in. Burton and I should have come to you ourselves, long ago. Don't blame us too much. We tried so hard to keep out of it. There wasn't any use."

Her shoulders were sagging as she turned to lead the way to the house. Al climbed out of the car to follow her.

"Isabel," she called to me, with a touch of asperity, "don't sit in the car like a dummy. Come in too. You might as well hear this now, and save me the trouble of crying on your shoulder later."

"Really, Alice," I called back.

"Come in. If I go on shouting at you like this, the neighbors will think there's something funny going on."

So, reluctantly, and embarrassed, I climbed out of the car too, and went up the walk after them.

She showed us to chairs in her cheerful green and red living-room, and excused herself a moment.

"I'll get Burton," she explained. "He didn't go to the office today. We—we rather expected you."

I looked at Al uncomfortably. I was terribly worried. Her whole manner was too ominous to be reassuring. Al was frowning a little at the door through which she had gone. I wondered what he was thinking.

She brought Burton back with her. He was ill at ease, and not at all the aggressive, self-confident man I was familiar with. He shook hands with Al quietly, and sat down opposite him. Alice took a seat on the sofa beside me, and took my hand.

"We're at your disposal, Captain Branson," said Burton.

For a moment Al himself seemed a little unsure of himself.

"You understand why I have come," he began at last.

"I think I do. I don't know how much you know, or how much you suspect, or where your case stands. But I suppose it's inevitable that you'd turn up something sooner or later to bring our names into it. Before we begin, I think we'd better make one thing clear. My wife and I have discussed this business since Miss Marsh called last night, and we realize the only course is to be completely frank with you, and to try to hide nothing. If you hadn't come around this morning I'd decided to look you up."

"Your attitude is very wise, Mr. Trent, if I may say so. I wish half the witnesses in the usual case were as helpful and coopera-tive. Do I understand you want to make a statement?"

"In effect, yes."

"Then I suggest you come to headquarters with me, where it can be transcribed, and you can sign it."

"I shall be glad to." Burton hesitated a moment. "I'd like to save Alice that trouble, if I could. Couldn't we give you a sort of preliminary statement verbally, and then, if you like, I could come with you, without bothering my wife?"

"Go ahead, Mr. Trent," Al directed. "If it's possible, I'll take her statement here."

"Thanks." Burton folded his hands around one knee. "I'm finding it hard to begin," he apologized.

"You knew Frank Murdock and the former Mrs. Murdock in the East, didn't you?" Al asked helpfully.

"Yes. Fairly well. We all saw something of each other and—" He cleared his throat and looked down at the carpet. Alice suddenly squeezed my hand.

"What you're both trying to get at, and are both being very gentlemanly about," Alice said abruptly, "is how well I knew Frank."

They both looked at her without comment. She flushed a little and drew her hand away from mine.

"Look, Captain Branson," she went on, "we've decided to be candid about it. I was very fond of Frank, or thought I was. Infatuated would probably be a better word. Now—now that he's gone I don't understand it myself. Women, sometimes, are attracted to men like that, blindly and foolishly. That's what you wanted to know, isn't it?"

"Yes," said Al, and looked decidedly uncomfortable. He set his jaw determinedly. "It is not always a pleasant job we do, Mrs. Trent. But we have to do it."

"Don't apologize. *I* wouldn't be paid to do it, but it's necessary work. We understand. Let's not beat around the bush. I thought I was in love with Frank. Now I see I wasn't, really. He appealed to me and I sympathized with him. I think Joan Craig was a worthless little tramp, and she wasn't giving Frank a break. If he came to me with most of his troubles, I couldn't help it. It flattered me. He was so darned good-looking. When he made love to me it—well, I don't care how much a woman cares for her husband, it tickles her vanity to know she's attractive to other men."

I studied Burton's face during this speech with some curiosity. He was embarrassed, but there was more than that in his expression. There was something that looked very much to me like pride and—well devotion. I suddenly realized that Burton worshipped Alice, for all his tempers and flare-ups. He was not hiding it.

"Tell me, Mrs. Trent: were you on, shall we say, these friendly terms with Mr. Murdock after he moved here?"

"Yes. Until—until he died."

"Were you aware of the fact that he intended to sue for alienation?"

"No. Emphatically not. That was one thing he didn't discuss with me, He probably knew what I'd think of it, and he didn't want to start a quarrel. I'd have been furious, and I think I might have changed my mind about him, if I'd known. I didn't know, either, that Mr. and Mrs. Emory were married. He didn't tell me that. Naturally we both expected them to marry, especially when Elaine—" She stopped and looked pleadingly at Burton, who was shaking his head vigorously. Al looked from one to the other.

"What about Elaine?" he said. "I thought there weren't to be any evasions or reservations."

"Oh, but this is—it's not—"

"What about Elaine?"

"She wasn't Frank's daughter," said Alice, in a low voice. I sat up, opened my mouth, and forgot to close it.

"How do you know?"

"Frank told me. He hadn't known it himself until he and Joan had a quarrel once. She called him all sorts of names, and then she told him."

"Did he know who the father was?"

"Well, it wouldn't take much arithmetic to figure out, you know. Joan refused to tell him that, and challenged him to divorce her. They had an awful quarrel. He never lived with her after that. But I think, down in his heart, he always carried a torch."

"Do you know who the father was?" Al was insistent.

"No. But if I hear of Thorne Emory adopting her, and having her name changed, I won't be surprised. Don't you see that's the real reason Frank was so bitter against Thorne?"

"I see. Yes. Now, Mrs. Trent, I have a rather personal question to ask. Did you, Mr. Trent, know how Mrs. Trent felt toward Mr. Murdock?"

There was a heavy silence for a moment. Then he answered thickly, "Yes. I discovered it a week or so ago."

I wanted desperately to get up and leave, to walk out in the garden, to do anything to get away. But I could not move. I waited through a long pause.

"He didn't tell me he'd known until last night," said Alice, and she sighed. I thought, for a moment, that she was going to cry. But she got up suddenly, and crossed to Burton's chair and sat down on the arm of it, her arm caressingly on his shoulders. "I was a fool! Such a fool!"

Burton grinned a little sheepishly, and patted her arm. There was a strained lightness in his voice as he addressed Al.

"It was one of those things, Captain, that loom so big, and mean so darned little, really. I guess we were both foolish. Oh, well, let's skip that. It's over and forgotten."

Al sighed and rubbed his thumb reflectively over his nose.

"I hope so," he said. "But I've still got my job to do. Mr. Trent, were you anywhere near the Emory house Thursday night?"

Burton replied without hesitation.

"Yes. I was."

I don't think Al expected that. He cast a speculative look at Burton before he continued his questioning.

"I wish you'd tell me the circumstances," he said, looking down at his folded hands.

"I'll have to go back," said Burton, "to the night before. Wednesday night, in fact. That night I wasn't at the office. Instead I called on Frank Murdock."

"You knew where he lived?" Al interrupted to ask.

"I heard my wife telephone him. His number, you know, isn't an extended service number, and it can't be dialled from the house here. She had to ask the operator, and I overheard it. She wasn't aware that I was in the house. So Wednesday I called Frank up and asked him to see me. He told me to meet him at his apartment, and I did.

"I don't suppose it's necessary for me to tell you why I went. I don't know exactly what I intended doing. The only thing I was sure of was that I had no intention of leaving there until I was certain that Frank would stop visiting my wife."

"You saw him Wednesday night?"

Burton nodded.

"Yes. The interview was a lot friendlier than I'd expected. I never cared very much for Frank. But he behaved pretty well. I don't have to go into detail, I suppose. He made certain promises easily enough, and I believed him. We settled the matter amicably."

I pictured that interview, as he described it, guessing at what he omitted: Frank's assurance that his feeling for Alice was platonic, probably apologizing for putting her in an awkward situation without meaning to, his promise to avoid repeating it, now that he realized the unfortunate consequences of what had been intended merely as friendliness. Frank, I remembered, had always been a suave, persuasive sort of person, with a great deal of charm to make up for a lack of more sterling virtues. Possibly, on returning home, Burton might have been less certain of Frank's sincerity; but at the time he might easily have been convinced.

"That was when he offered me a highball and we drank to better understanding. All very chummy," Burton repeated. "And I'd cooled down a lot by then, and we sat around and talked for a while."

"Was his brother there?" Al asked.

"No. I didn't see James. Frank was alone.

"Well, he told me then that he had decided to sue Emory for alienation. I was a bit surprised. I mean, you don't do things like that. Granted that he had a case, I'm not sure Emory was entirely to blame for the situation that had grown up between Frank and his wife. I always felt the marriage was a mistake anyway.

"I tried to talk him out of it. I might have saved my breath. He made it plain it wasn't any affair of mine. So I left, still on good terms, but pretty disgusted.

"As I said, that was Wednesday evening. Thursday I telephoned Emory. Frank had told me he and Joan were living in Bel-Air, and I called him. I'd been associated with Emory on some business deals a couple of years ago, and I made a purely social phone call, asking them both to dinner some evening. What Emory told me over the phone surprised me a good deal.

"He asked me if I'd heard about the suit, and I told him I had. He wasn't at all friendly. He was, in fact, pretty hard-boiled, and I resented his tone from the beginning. I've thought it over since, and I believe now that he was deliberately cold about it as a salve to his conscience. I don't remember his exact words over the phone, but he did tell me that he had every intention of fighting the case against Frank with every means at his command. He had flatly refused to settle out of court because of the risks. He realized, he told me, that if any hint ever leaked out that he had settled such an issue that way, it would be an admission of guilt and would damage his reputation. *He* had to take it to court and be completely vindicated.

"I said something about the damage the publicity of a trial

would do, and he agreed that it might. But he considered it the lesser risk. He felt sure of a vindication, and he repeated that he would use every means to gain it. Even, he said, if some damage were done to other reputations. 'After all, Burton,' he said, 'I'm not responsible for other people's indiscretions. I'm sorry, but if they've been foolish, it's up to them to cover their own sins.''

"It was pretty obvious what he meant. 'I've had detectives following Murdock,' he said, to make it even more clear. 'I don't think there'd be much trouble scraping up enough evidence to show that Frank's hands weren't so spotless that he could afford to bring suit.'

"Naturally anything Frank had done since the divorce made very little real difference to the case. But it just happened that Frank had called on my wife several times before we left for California, and I knew it, and I was convinced Emory knew it and had proof of it. I asked Emory to consider what he was doing.

" 'I think I have,' he said firmly. So I asked him if I could see him and discuss the matter. He told me to come around that evening. He'd have to see his lawyer for a short time, but he'd be home early, and he'd be willing to talk to me. But he emphasized the fact that he considered an interview a waste of time. I insisted. So we set the appointment, and I hung up.

"I must have been in a blue funk the rest of the morning. I had straightened out an awkward situation to satisfy myself, but apparently that wasn't enough. In a way I am as vulnerable to publicity as Emory. More so, I think, because I have political ambitions, and frankly, Captain Branson, any scandal is pretty fatal to a candidate for public office."

"Do you believe Emory actually intended to drag your wife through a public exposure?" Al asked.

"Emory's case, it seems to me, was so weak that he could only hope to win it by showing that the original fault lay with Frank. In the divorce, of course, that wasn't necessary. Grounds for divorce in Reno are less limited. Desertion, non-support, incompatibility, cruelty—anything like that. Naturally Joan should have sued on stronger grounds. Then they might have spiked Frank's guns to begin with. I don't think they realized the danger of Frank's actually bringing suit, though, until too late.

"I'm explaining this pretty fully, because I want you to realize my position exactly. I want you to see precisely why I did what I did.

"I was supposed to meet Emory that evening, for what promised to be a nasty, and probably useless, interview. I couldn't expect cooperation from him. It was up to me to do something myself if I wanted to stall off a mess of trouble.

"Well, money talks. I called Frank and offered him one hundred thousand dollars to call off his suit."

## *Chapter* XXI

AL DID not, by so much as a flicker of his eyelids, betray any surprise, but I gasped, audibly, in the silence that fell. Burton looked at me and shrugged a little.

"Probably it was foolish. But what else could I do?"

"But what did Frank say?" I demanded. "Burton, what did he say?"

"He wouldn't hear of it. It wasn't the money, he said, it was the principle of the thing. But I wasn't finished. I went over to his place Thursday afternoon, with the cash."

"Could you raise that amount so quickly?"

"Yes. I have a fairly large balance in several banks, and a large amount in negotiable securities. Between the two, I was able to get the money together by that afternoon. I thought the sight of that amount in cash would have more effect on him than any amount of talking."

"Did you see him?" Al asked.

"Yes. And to be honest about it, Frank was a lot more reasonable than Emory had been. He understood my position.

" 'I'm sorry,' he said. 'I hadn't realized how other people might be hurt, but I've been thinking it over.' But he still insisted that it would not suit him to drop proceedings without some substantial return. 'I tell you what I'll do,' he said. 'I'll agree to drop the case, and accept this on one condition.' I asked him what that condition was, and he explained. 'I want to handle this my own way. I won't agree to drop out right away, but I promise you to keep things out of court. That will save you publicity. But I've got my counselor's fees to pay in any case, and I want to throw a scare into Emory. Maybe I can get him to settle. If I can't, I think I can work on Joan. I'm going to try that first.'

"Well, we argued the point. I didn't want to take even that risk, but he wouldn't consider any other terms. I was forced to agree. I told him I'd pay him the one hundred thousand the moment he withdrew his suit, and that I would sign an agreement to that effect.

"Then there was another argument. With the money in front of him, he couldn't bear to see me take it away again.

" 'I tell you what I'll do,' he said finally. 'You leave this with me. I'll give you a letter to my lawyer dated one week from today, withdrawing the suit against the Emories, signed and ready to be mailed. If you don't hear from me in the meantime, you're free to mail it. I'm going to see Joan tonight, and if I'm successful, I'll call you at once, and give the lawyer personal instructions tomorrow. You can destroy the letter then.'

"I agreed to that, with one other proposal as a condition. He would give me a thirty-day note for one hundred thousand dollars in addition to the letter, as a safeguard.

"That seemed to be satisfactory to him, provided a third person held the note. He wasn't taking any chances that I might try to collect on the note after he had fulfilled his part of the bargain. Anyway, he wrote the letter to his lawyer—I have it in my safe at the office and I'll be glad to show it to you—and signed the note, which he enclosed in a sealed envelope and mailed, with a covering letter, to his attorney. The letter instructed the lawyer—Post, I think his name is—to destroy the enclosure without breaking its seal one week from that day, or at any time before then that steps were taken to drop the case against Emory.

"I left, then, and he promised to call me late that night and tell me what had happened when he'd seen Joan.

"I had dinner with a friend of mine, Mr. Wood, and right afterwards I left him, and drove over to the Emory house. I had little hope of gaining anything by seeing Emory, but I still wanted to talk to him, and try to persuade him to settle the matter with Frank. I had Frank's word he would drop the whole business, of course, but I'm not sure I trusted him. After all, he could have asked Post to destroy that note at any time, and countermanded any instructions as to the halting of the alienation proceedings. If Emory chose to be hard about it, Frank could easily have taken that course, and had me in a worse position than I was in before. Out one hundred thousand dollars.

"I had to trust him, even with the safeguards I'd taken. When

I thought it over, I saw that they weren't so much of an insurance of good faith as I'd have liked.

"Well, when I got to the Emories' house I saw Miss Marsh's car parked there, as well as Frank's car, and I hesitated about ringing the bell. I decided to wait in my own car until Frank left. Then I saw a police car coming along the street.

"There have been several tire thefts lately in the darker parts of town, and the police have stopped me once or twice when I've been driving at night. I knew they'd question me if I was sitting in my car, and I decided it would be better to wait in the grounds. So I went into the yard, and walked around to the back, trying to see whether or not Frank was leaving.

"The ground floor was dark except for a light in the kitchen, but there was a light in an upstairs room that I could see from the path in back. The shades weren't drawn, and Joan and Frank were talking together near the window. I saw them clearly. I don't know where Miss Marsh was. I didn't see her."

"I was watching you from the living-room," I said, before Al could stop me. "I had the light out. And you had me scared to death. Burton, don't tell me you shot Frank!"

Burton looked at me with a faint smile.

"No," he said. "I didn't shoot him. When I saw Joan and Frank together, and didn't see Emory anywhere, I decided he hadn't come home yet. I started back toward the front of the house to wait for him there. The shrubbery was pretty thick around there, and I walked around the kitchen end where it was much thinner. I passed the garage, and saw Emory's car there. He'd evidently just come in.

"So I went toward the front door, meaning to wait until Frank left and then ring. But there was a man standing at the front door."

"A man?" Al asked. "Do you know who he was?"

"No. It was too dark to see. The trees keep out almost all the light from the street lights. Once he pushed open the peephole in the door. You've probably seen that peephole yourself. It's about eight inches square, with a pane of frosted glass in it. It opens inward. Evidently it wasn't fastened, because the man, whoever he was, pushed it open and looked into the hall. But the hall was dark, too, and there wasn't enough light shining out to show me who he was.

"The man's actions were so odd that I stood there watching for a minute. Then I decided it was none of my business anyway and

I walked down to the gate. The police car had gone long ago, and I went out to sit in my car. From where it was parked I could see Frank's car still standing there.

"I looked at my watch and saw it was getting late. I was due over at Mr. Wood's pretty soon, and it looked as if Frank might be in there a long time. So I decided to call the thing off for the evening and reach Emory the next morning. I drove off, and went out to Mr. Wood's.

"The next morning I read about Frank's murder in the paper, and I decided the only thing to do was to sit tight and see what happened. If I volunteered any information, I knew I'd have to tell the whole story, and I didn't want to do that. It would mean dragging out the affair between Frank and my wife, and the business of that hundred thousand that would certainly look peculiar and be hard to explain.

"Since I hadn't called at the house I didn't see any reason why Emory should mention my appointment with him, and I hoped he wouldn't. Besides, he had no way of knowing whether I'd tried to keep it. It was possible and even likely that I wouldn't be connected with it in any way. The only thing I had to worry about was that note of Frank's in the sealed envelope. There was a chance that Post would go to the police with that. But I had to risk that.

"So there you are, Captain Branson."

Al rearranged himself in his chair.

"You realize, Mr. Trent," he said, "that your story does not clear you of any suspicion. I have so far only your unsupported word on the whole thing."

"I know that, yes. I have Frank's letter to Post, however."

"If you had reason to believe you could not hold Murdock to his agreement, the letter is worthless. I'm sorry. It only helps to establish a motive. The only way you could be certain the suit would be dropped would be if Frank were dead. I have to point that out to you. You have no witness to prove you left the house before Murdock was shot. Did you, by the way, hear the shot?"

"No. I did not. I must have left before then."

"How long would it take you to drive from the Emory house to Mr. Wood's?"

"About ten minutes. But I didn't drive along Sunset Boulevard. I tried some of the roads in Bel-Air. I thought they'd be shorter, but I became confused. Those roads twist and turn like snakes. It took me a good twenty-five minutes to get there."

"So you have no proof that you left before the murder. The story you tell of another man at the door is curious, but you have no proof of that either."

"No, I admit I haven't."

"There was no trace of the hundred thousand dollars you claim to have left with Frank that afternoon. I gather it was too late then for him to deposit it. The banks were already closed. We've examined Murdock's effects, and that money and the securities weren't among them. Frank may have hidden them somewhere, but I don't know where."

"James might know."

"Possibly. He did not volunteer the information, however."

"I doubt if he even knew about it," said Burton. "I believe Frank owed him money. He wouldn't be apt to tell him he had that amount for fear James would want him to repay him."

"That's possible too. In the meantime I have no choice but to put you under arrest. You see that, I hope."

Burton nodded. Alice, still seated on the arm of his chair, put her arm around him protectingly.

"He didn't do it; oh, can't you see he wouldn't do a thing like that?" she cried.

"I'm sorry," said Al inexorably. I could say nothing. Al was right. "By the way, Mrs. Trent, did Frank Murdock at any time lend you his gun? A Colt .25?"

I'm quite sure he couldn't have expected her to admit it. What he wanted was her reaction to the question: a start of guilty surprise, something like that. Or perhaps he wanted to give her that chance to help Burt by telling him that someone else had the gun.

"No, I never even knew he had one," she said dully.

Al rose.

"I'll have to ask you to come with me, Mr. Trent. I have no warrant for your arrest, but I think you see I'll have no difficulty getting one. It will be easier if you'd come at once, and waive formality."

"Of course." He rose, too, his heavy frame moving sluggishly, as if he could hardly control it.

Alice looked like a pale ghost.

"Please!" she begged, her hand holding tight to Burton's arm. "Captain Branson, you can't do this. Listen. Doris Ayers was killed last night, wasn't she?"

Al paused.

"Yes," he said, looking at her with sympathetic interest.

"You believe, don't you, that the person who killed Frank killed her too?"

"We believe so."

"Then Burton couldn't have done it! He was here with me all evening."

"You'd have to prove that, Mrs. Trent."

"I can. I can very easily. From seven o'clock on we entertained friends of ours, a Mr. and Mrs. Norris, for dinner and bridge. They left here at eleven."

Al looked to Burton for confirmation.

"That's true," he said.

Al hesitated.

"I think I'll have to ask you to come anyway," he said at last. "That eliminates you for last night, but it doesn't alter the situation with regard to Thursday night. You see, we don't know that Miss Ayers was killed by the same person. It's quite possible that she was not."

## *Chapter* XXII

I STAYED with Alice for quite a while after Al had taken Burton away. She was dry-eyed but frightfully upset, blaming herself for the position she had put Burton in; and his loyalty to her and his sympathetic understanding hadn't helped her. If anything, it made things worse, and she indulged in an orgy of self-abeg- it made things worse.

"But you know he had nothing to do with it, don't you, Isabel?" she repeated at intervals. "You know that. They'll let him come home, won't they?"

I reassured her as well as I could, though that, too, did little to help her. I finally persuaded her to try to work in the garden and take her mind off the matter.

"You know Al Branson won't let anything happen to Burt," I said. "You know Burton told the truth, and Al will be convinced of it, too, as soon as he checks up on it. But he had to take Burt along, on the evidence. There wasn't anything else he could do."

"I know. I know," she murmured. "But if I hadn't been such a fool—"

I left her, finally, though I hated to. But that spot of mud on Joan's bedroom floor was still bothering me, and I was beginning to form a theory about it.

It was only a short walk from Alice's to my own house, where I picked up my car, after I'd eaten the light lunch Fern had waiting for me. Then I drove to Wilshire Boulevard, and went to a movie.

It seemed a heartless thing to be doing, and I hoped no one I knew would see me slip in. I parked the car in an empty lot next to the theater, and bought my ticket at the window. I did not even notice what pictures were playing, and when the usherette led me to a seat on the side, I sat for a moment or two clutching my ticket stub; and staring, almost without consciousness, at the screen where two comedians, one fat and one thin, were driving madly down twisting mountain roads in a Ford, pursued by Indians. The audience was swept by waves of uproarious laughter.

I watched the frantic chase for about ten minutes, until the Ford had crashed completely through a frame house, emerging with an iron bedstead in front of it, in which an old man with a night-cap was presumably sleeping soundly. I did not stop to ponder why he was in bed at what was obviously about mid-day. I waited until the laughter was loud, rose, and pushed my way past empty seats to the side aisle.

A large door there bore the word "exit" over it, and I pushed experimentally against it. It swung open, and admitted me into a dim corridor with another door at the end of it. This door, I found, opened into an alley beside the theater, on the side opposite the parking lot.

I let the door close behind me, and walked down the alley for a few steps. At the far end was a street running parallel with Wilshire Boulevard, but I did not bother to explore further. I returned to the heavy door, and tried to open it. I was afraid, for a moment, that I might not find a handle on the outside, but there was one, and I reentered the corridor, and opened the second door into the theater.

Almost immediately, as I expected, there was an usherette at my side, flashing a light in my face.

"I'm sorry, Madam," she said stormily, "you can't come in this way."

I held out my ticket stub to her, and she focussed her floodlight on it.

"I just remembered," I explained glibly to her, "that I'd left the keys of my car in the ignition lock. I was afraid to leave them there, and I went out to get them."

"Well," the usher said, dubiously, "you hadn't ought to go out that way, Madam. If you'd told the man at the door he'd have let you through. I'm supposed to report you."

"I'm sorry," I said, contritely. "I won't do it again. You can see from my stub I just came in."

"All right, Madam," she said with bored finality, and vanished up the aisle in a swirl of red satin slacks. I went back to my seat, and watched the two comedians, one of them now disguised as an Indian, the other, unaccountably, as a veiled harem beauty, riding horses amid a throng of other Indians. The fat one was laughing cherubically at some joke hidden from me, and it was never revealed, for at that moment the words, "The End," flashed upon the screen. A moment or two later several people rose and began to leave the theater in what I'm sure the usherette would have considered the proper manner. I mingled with them, praying that she would not notice me, and report me to the management, who would surely have me sent to the psychopathic ward for observation, if she had anything to say about it.

It was still very early in the afternoon when I emerged from my brief glimpse of the movies, and I reflected, for a moment, on the contribution I had made to the war effort for four cents in amusement taxes, and tried not to be too complacent about it. But I had found out what I wanted to know, and I went back to my car with a certain sense of elation.

I knew Al would not approve of my interfering in any way in the solution of the murders, but I could hardly see how even he could object to my merely going to a movie.

As soon as I reached home I called Joan and asked if I could see her. She consented, rather ungraciously.

"Reporters and detectives and everything else are driving me crazy," she said. "If I didn't stay in bed I'd be mauled to death. I wish the police would hurry up and end this whole business, Isabel. I feel like a prisoner quarantined or something."

"I'm sure you do," I said sympathetically. "I thought I might cheer you up a little."

"That's nice of you. Yes, come over. Say, right after dinner."

"Fine. See you then," I said.

I waited rather impatiently until seven-thirty, a period that was relieved only by a call from Al, at five. He was rather apologetic.

"I hope you understand why I had to arrest Trent," he said. "There wasn't anything else to do."

"I know. Do you really suspect him, Al? You can't really."

"Perhaps I can't, as you say. But, Isabel, I can't go around patting all our suspects on the back just because you're sure they didn't do it, or because I happen to like them."

"Well, tell me this. Have you found out anything to prove he was telling the truth?"

"Only knowing the whole truth will help us there. However," he added, "I've been with Thaddeus Post most of the day, and he's denied absolutely that he received any sealed envelope from Frank. And he can't tell us anything about the hundred thousand dollars. Frank certainly didn't leave it with him for safekeeping."

"Anything else?"

"I've been checking time with Wood. And the Norrises say they spent the evening with the Trents last night. Burton at least wasn't out of their sight from about seven until eleven. Mrs. Trent was on the phone several times, but she was in the house. And there's no trace of a taxi taking anyone to Bel-Air Thursday night."

"When am I going to see you?"

"I don't know," he said, and he sounded tired. "I'll probably be busy for hours. Are you behaving?"

"Of course. I went to the movies this afternoon."

"Good," he said abstractedly; "take your mind off things."

"That's what I thought. Tonight I'm going over to sit with Joan awhile. You don't mind that, do you?"

"Joan Emory? I thought you hated the sight of her."

"She's nervous, Al. And I don't think she has many friends."

"All right. All right. But be home early, and watch out. But you'll probably be all right. I don't think anything more is apt to happen there. But be sure to have somebody with you all the time. On second thought—"

"I'll be all right, Al," I said hastily, and hung up before he could complete his second thought.

I left for Joan's, however, without trepidation. The safe streets of Beverly Hills, so well patrolled by such thoroughly efficient and pleasant police, give one a sense of security that made me incautious. It was only when I was near the circle opposite the Emories' that I began to feel, once more, that disturbing little fear that I always felt around that house.

I drove into the grounds and parked in front of the garage. O'Hara was in the yard, and that reassured me.

"I'm going in the back way," I said to him, "whether I shock everybody or not, O'Hara. I don't like that dark front path."

"Can't say as I blame you, Miss Marsh," he said, with a friendly grin. He pushed the kitchen door open for me, and ushered me in. Sarah and the cook were in the kitchen, finishing the dishes.

"Are Mr. and Mrs. Emory at home?" I asked.

Sarah wiped her hands on a towel.

"Mr. Emory had to go out," she said, "but you can go right up to Mrs. Emory's room, Miss Marsh."

I went through the dark dining-room, into the hall where the amber light burned in the one lamp over the stairs. The living-room and library were both dark, and I hurried toward the steps, with one glimpse toward the front door and its peephole.

Elaine was in Joan's bedroom with her. It was the first time I had seen her in years, and I was surprised at how she had grown. But more astonishing still was her strong resemblance to Frank Murdock. Her hair was very dark, and she had Frank's dark, handsome eyes, softened, in Elaine, to warm friendliness. Her lips, too, were the fine chiselled Murdock lips. Whatever Alice had thought about Elaine's parentage there was no question about it in my mind the instant I looked at her. Frank must have lied about that.

Joan treated her with a sort of aloof playfulness. We talked and laughed for a while, over really nothing at all. But the moment Joan became bored, she told Elaine to run along and find Sarah. Elaine, evidently used to abrupt dismissals, merely said "Yes, Mummy. Goood night, Aunt Isabel," and went obediently.

"I'm glad you called," Joan said after Elaine had disappeared. "I'm lonely, and Thorne's out with that attorney of his. If this business isn't ended pretty soon, Isabel, I'll go crazy."

"It will be over soon, Joan. Do you know they arrested Burton Trent today?"

"*Burton!* Oh, no!"

"They certainly did. He was the man I saw out in the yard that night."

Joan stared at me unbelievingly.

"You're crazy, Isabel! Burt no more killed Frank than—than Elaine did."

"I know he didn't. But he was outside there when it happened."

"Did he see anything?" she asked.

"No. I think he'd already left by the time Frank was shot. But the trouble is he can't prove it. Joan, we've got to help Burt."

"I'd be only too glad to help him, Isabel, but I wouldn't know how. I told that policeman of yours everything I knew."

"I'm sure you did," I exclaimed diplomatically. "But you know, Joan, there might be some little something you've overlooked. Are you sure there isn't?"

"Positive."

"You know, Burton says he saw someone looking in through the peephole in the front door just before the shot was fired."

"He did?" She looked puzzled. "A man?"

"Yes."

"Did he know who it was?"

"No. He couldn't see him well enough. You know, Joan, the police have been curious to figure out how people got here that night. Burton, for instance, and so on. They've checked up on whether anybody came out in taxis or buses or anything like that. I'm wondering if by any chance somebody came here in Frank's car with him. Did he mention anything like that to you when you talked to him?"

She thumped her pillows into a more comfortable position.

"No. What are you getting at, Isabel?"

"Nothing particular. I'm just trying to put things together a little." I was sitting by the dressing-table, and I picked up her lipstick and began inspecting it idly. "For instance," I said, in as casual a tone as I could, "I'm wondering where you went last night."

"I? You're crazy. I didn't leave the room."

I smiled at her knowingly.

"Oh, I wasn't going to give you away, Joan," I said. "But after all, I couldn't help seeing your shoes had fresh mud on them."

She looked at me silently for several moments, her eyes narrowed, trying, I suppose, to decide just what I was up to.

"You're dreaming," she declared at last, but she did not look at me.

"No. I saw them. So did Captain Branson."

"Well," she said, "after all, I have to get *some* air. I can't sit here all day long. After it got dark I took a short walk in the garden. Why shouldn't I?"

"No reason at all, of course. But I don't think Captain Branson would be convinced of that."

"I don't care. That's all it was," she said.

"He'll probably plague you tomorrow until you tell him," I warned her.

She shrugged. "Well, I wish him luck."

"So do I. Joan, where did you really go? You know it was just about then that Doris was killed. It looks awful for you. Just like Burton's being here the night before does for him."

She was distinctly uneasy; I could see that.

"Isabel, you're just being silly. You think, because you have a friend in the Homicide Squad, that you're a detective or something. Grow up."

"Oh, very well, if you don't want to tell me. But, Joan, you know it does look funny."

"All right," she said, suddenly capitulating. "I did go downstairs for a minute or two. But it had nothing to do with Doris. I swear to that."

"Yes?" I said, unconvinced.

"I see I'll have to tell you just to keep you quiet. I might have known you'd see those shoes. You always were nosy. But you must keep that policeman from knowing. I've beeen annoyed enough already."

I said nothing. If she expected me to promise to keep what she told me to myself, she was disappointed. I waited quietly for her to go on.

"Isabel, you probably won't believe a word I say. But this is the truth. I went downstairs to see someone. You see, I knew the police would be looking through all of Frank's papers. Well, among those papers were some letters I'd received. Thorne wrote them to me from time to time long before I divorced Frank. I guess it was foolish of me to keep them. But I didn't dream at the time that they'd ever be dangerous. As a matter of fact, I really forgot about them. But Frank must have found them in my bureau once, during one of the few times he was at home.

"Don't you see that they'd be misinterpreted if anyone else saw them? Frank was going to use them at the trial."

"It seems to me, Joan, you practically brought this whole business on yourself," I said. "You practically threw Thorne at

Frank's head. You couldn't expect him not to resent it, you know."

"I know," she admitted. "But he used to annoy me so. I wanted to hurt him. Does that sound catty of me? Well, I can't help if it does. I wanted to." Her voice had taken on a bitter quality. Her fingers were clenched together on the violet comfort, and her knuckles were pink from the pressure.

"Sometimes you went pretty far, didn't you?" I asked pointedly. "About Elaine, I mean."

She glanced at me with something like alarm in her eyes.

"Who told you that?" she demanded.

"Never mind. I knew it."

"But it wasn't true. It wasn't true at all, Isabel! I couldn't tell Frank the truth."

For a moment I was completely at a loss. Joan's last remark simply did not make sense, if she had lied to Frank about Elaine. After all, in my experience I had never heard of a woman trying to hide from her husband the fact of his parentage. And Elaine was so obviously a Murdock. So obviously—

I dropped Joan's lipstick on the floor, and had to grope for it, in my confusion. I was as pink as a radish when I sat up again. It was all clear to me now why James had helped support Joan all those years without complaint. For a moment I felt a little sorry for Joan. She had made such an unholy mess of her life. But that sympathy died almost at once, and I looked at her with something like horrified disgust. It must have shown in my face; because she turned away uncomfortably. I caught just the glimpse of tears in her eyes.

"Don't look at me like that, Isabel! I had so little happiness. Can you blame me for taking it when I could?"

"Joan, I'm not judging anybody. I wish—I wish I hadn't even mentioned the subject. I want to forget it. It seems to me we were talking about some letters. Let's stick to that."

She dabbed at her eyes with a little lace handkerchief.

"I don't know why I'm telling you any of this," she remarked, "except that it would look so much worse if it were dragged out of me. But Thorne would never forgive me if he knew I'd told you. You see, Frank had those letters, and I couldn't let them fall into the hands of the police."

"How did you know Frank had them?"

"He told me, Thursday night when he was here. Yesterday James called up and told me he'd got hold of them, and kept them

from the police. He asked me if I wanted him to destroy them.
But I know Thorne didn't trust James for a minute, and I told
him I'd rather have them myself, and let Thorne destroy them.
Then he'd be sure they'd never be published in the newspapers
or anything like that.

"James said it would be hard to bring them to me without
arousing suspicion, because a detective was following him. But he
thought he could manage it by being seen going into a movie, and
then sneaking out a side door. I told him I'd meet him down in
the yard around half-past eight.

"And then, of course, Captain Branson came back with Thorne
and almost spoiled it all. When Thorne came up to the room I
told him, and he told me to slip down the back steps. He promised
to keep Captain Branson busy in the living-room long enough for
me to get the letters from James and sneak back up again.

"And, Isabel, I swear that's all that happened."

"You met James out by the pepper tree?" I asked.

"Yes. He had the letters and gave them to me. What he did
after that I don't know. I slipped back into the house and had just
got back into bed when you came in. I didn't even have time
to put the shoes away."

"Do you know when Doris went out, Joan?"

"Why, yes," she said promptly. "It was about ten minutes before. She came into the room with her hat on and asked if I'd mind
if she went out for a short walk. I told her to go ahead."

I shook my head because it had begun to spin.

"Joan, how did James act when you met him? Was he excited,
or anything like that?"

"James?" Her eyes widened, and she stared at me for a moment before she answered. I saw dawning comprehnsion in her
eyes. "No. He was—just himself, Isabel. I didn't notice anything,
but I was rather excited myself, and so I might not have noticed.
He said he'd been waiting for quite a while. He'd hidden himself
when Thorne and Captain Branson came in."

It was all clear to me now; I was positive that I knew what
had happened that night. There were just two points which were
not quite established. Joan could, I felt sure, settle one point.

"Where did James hide while Thorne was coming in?" I asked
eagerly. My tenseness must have communicated itself to Joan,
because she sat up straight in her bed, her eyes bright and sharp.

"He said he'd waited behind the garage for ten or fifteen minutes."

"But he was waiting under the pepper trees near the gate when you met him?"

"Yes. He said he'd noticed that there was some kind of excitement going on in the house and he'd been afraid I wasn't going to be able to meet him. He was just getting ready to leave when he saw me. In fact, he'd almost reached the gate, and he turned back when he saw me."

"Do you think he was telling the truth, Joan?"

"I did then. Now, I wonder."

## *Chapter* XXIII

"**B**UT you see, don't you," asked Joan, with the odd intensity that had come into her manner, "that it wouldn't do for the police to pry into that? I couldn't explain meeting James, so they'd understand it. And if they knew I'd been out just about the time Doris—but she must have been dead already then, mustn't she?"

I got up, and straightened my hat.

"Yes. It was probably later when you went down. Joan, it's getting late, and I'm going home. I'm tired. I wish to heaven I hadn't come over here Thursday night. But that can't be helped now."

"No, it can't," she agreed. She held out her hand to me, and there was a trace of warmth in her voice as she added, "But you were a help, Isabel. Really you were."

My mind wasn't really on what I was saying. There was one thing more I had to know, and I couldn't see how I could find out. It was one of those things no one would tell me, because only the murderer and one other person would know, and that other person must not suspect that I was interested.

I said goodbye and walked slowly down the steps, wondering what I could do to obtain the information I needed.

Sarah Bentley was in the lower hall, ready to show me out.

"I've just put Miss Elaine to bed," she said conversationally. "She's that upset about Miss Ayers, Miss Marsh. I think she cared more for her than she did for her own mother."

"Does she know that Miss Ayers was—was killed?" I asked, pausing at the door.

"No, indeed!" said Sarah. "She believes she's gone home. But I think she knows something strange happened, it was so sudden."

"I know," I murmured sympathetically. "Did Miss Ayers have any family, Sarah? I suppose it will be a shock for them."

"That it will! She had a mother living in a town called Painter, in Ohio, or somewhere around there. I've been busy packing her things to send there, and it almost breaks my heart doing it, her things so neat and all, and her room just like she left it, one of her blue dresses tossed on the bed, and her toilet articles all laid out neat as pins on the dressing table. It does give you more of a turn seeing a person's belongings after they're gone than even going to the funeral, I think."

"You're right, Sarah. I've always felt that way, too. Sarah, I wonder if you could tell me something. If you're standing behind the garage, can you see the kitchen door?"

"No, Miss Marsh. The garage, really, is part of the house, though you can't get into it from the house. It's right under the cook's room, and it opens out to the side, same as the kitchen door does. Back of it is a little woodshed, and then all those winding paths and the barranca. You couldn't see the kitchen at all from there."

"Thank you." I went to the door, which she held open for me. A cool damp wind was blowing, and the bright sky was overcast.

"Mind you take care going home," Sarah warned me. She closed the door behind me, and I started along that fiendish path, where the pepper trees hung down, brushing against my head like soft, restraining fingers.

A floodlight burned over the garage door, lighting the driveway, making it brighter than I had ever seen it before, for which I was grateful. I think, too, that was what tempted me to look behind the garage.

In itself it was a trifling thing, and hardly to be considered dangerous. But it almost cost me my life.

I saw what I wanted to see—that, if Frank had stood there he was not only out of sight of anyone at the kitchen end of the

house, but that he was unable to see anything that happened there
as well.

I should have let it go at that. The floodlight did not reach that
thickly grown back of the house, and it was dark there. But I was
still curious, and anxious to see the library door from outside.

I passed the dining-room windows, which opened on the back,
and the row of windows in the library wall, all uncurtained, as I
could tell by the faint reflection of the hall light coming through
them. The door was next, and I tried it. It was solidly locked, so
I put my nose against a pane of the glass and looked in.

I found I could not see the steps at all. My view included only
the wall beside the steps, with the door leading down to the cellar.

I shrugged and gave up. Sleuthing back there in a thicket crawl-
ing with snails and worse did not appeal to me, and I decided to
go away at once. It was shorter, now, to continue on around the
house and come out by the walk that led past the badminton court.
From there I could follow the lighted street back to the driveway
and my car.

But when I turned to do that, something went wrong. I stepped
too far back, and tripped over the bricks edging the gravel walk.
Beyond them the ground dropped sharply to the barranca, and I
felt myself falling, without the level ground under my feet that I
had expected.

It was a nasty fall, with jagged branches clawing at me as I
plunged through. I struck soft ground and slid until I struck the
trunk of a eucalyptus tree, and stopped, breathless and shocked.
For a moment I lay perfectly still, convinced that I was too in-
jured to do anything else. Then I began to draw in gulping breaths
of air and be conscious of more localized pain.

I began to move myself cautiously. Everything seemed to be
still in one piece, even if I was covered with a hundred bruises.
But my knee ached abominably. I could hardly bend it. I sat there
rubbing it, and wincing every time my fingers touched it.

I sat there for several minutes, trying to calm a rising feeling
of helpless panic. I knew I hadn't broken any bones, and if I
waited a few minutes more I could probably totter back to the car
without too much pain. But somehow waiting there seemed the
most torturing thing in the world.

I don't know how long I sat there altogether. If I were comput-
ing the time I would say something like three hours. Actually it
could not have been much more than fifteen minutes. The knee

was better by then, and I stood up and tried putting weight on it.
It almost collapsed under me at first, but I got used to it, and I
tried limping up the pathway, which was a dark grey serpent
against black velvet.

My progress was slow and accompanied by many groans and
a few well chosen words of comfort. I got to the corner of the
house at last, and the large terrace, covered with an awning, that
extended from the living-room end.

And there I stood, resting a moment, when the night became
hideous with screaming sirens.

Almost at once the street lights went off, and a moment later
the light in Joan's bedroom, which had cast an oblong of yellow
radiance on the lawn, vanished. The sirens continued their nerve-
racking wail, rising and falling in pitch, like the dying scream of
a gargantuan monster.

It was too late to reach my car. I knew what those sirens meant
—air-raid blackout, total and complete, and no traffic on the
streets. The only thing I could do was to get into the house and
wait for the all clear. I prayed that Joan would have a room prepared with blackout curtains, because the prospect of being in
the darkness did not appeal to me at all.

I groped my way to the terrace, and across it to where the
door opened into the living-room. Already most of the city lights
had gone out, and the sky, which until then had been a murky,
luminous red from neons reflected on low clouds, was utterly
black. I have never seen such utter blackness. I could not see my
hand when I held it up. My eyes began to feel as if the blackness were actually pressing against them.

I barely crept toward the door, in fear of running into it unexpectedly. I held my hands out, feeling for something, and,
naturally, scraped against a flower pot hanging from the wall in
a metal bracket. It came loose and crashed down with a terrific
clatter, probably breaking into pieces.

Almost beside me a voice said, scarcely above a whisper,
"Who's there?"

"It's I," I said, my heart suddenly beginning to thump. "Isabel. Isabel Marsh. Who are you?"

There was no reply. Suddenly I felt cold, as cold as if I had
been coated with ice.

"Who are you?" I repeated. "Where?"

I heard a faint scraping sound near me, but that was all.

Someone was there, not four feet from me. The sound of breathing grew more plain, but the person did not answer.

I groped for the door, frightened out of my wits by now. My hand touched something that felt like a broom handle, and that slipped past my fingers and crashed down on the terrace floor. Before me was a blank stucco wall.

I had no idea where I was. I couldn't see anything. I have been in dark rooms before, but there has always been a little reflection somewhere, something that would show you where the walls were, or the doors. But here the blackness was complete. It was as black as it had been once when I was being taken through Endless Caverns in Virginia and the guide had extinguished the lights for a moment. My visible universe had ceased to exist. The faint breathing still reached me, but it came through solid darkness.

What prevented me, then and there, from going completely mad, I don't know. I should have been a gibbering idiot from that moment on. But somehow I clung to my sanity. I began to feel along the wall. The breathing seemed to come closer.

Then something released my voice which, until then, had simply failed to function.

"Joan!" I screamed. "Help me. Help me! I'm here!"

I know now that she did not hear me. She had gone into Elaine's room, at the far end of the house, and was sitting with her. No one heard me.

My knees wouldn't support me. I sank down to the icy tiles of the terrace, crouching against the wall. That breathing was still close, and with it the sounds of cautious footsteps, barely moving across the tiles.

I have never in my life before felt as helpless. The door may have been an inch from my fingers, but it might as well not have existed. There was no place to turn to, no way to escape. Around me was nothing but darkness, and it might be hours before light was restored.

If there had been a moon or stars I might have been able to see something, but the sky was clouded, and when I looked up it was impossible to see it. Little flecks of light seemed to jump across my eyes, confusing me.

Somehow I felt that if I could get into the house I would be safe. At least there would be someone there to cling to, someone who would answer when I spoke.

I crouched and felt along the wall. I did not even know which direction to follow. Everything was turned around completely for me.

And then I felt glass panes in a wooden frame, and I reached up, as quietly as I could, trying to find the door knob. It seemed minutes before I felt it, and closed my fingers around it. I turned it, and nothing happened. The door was locked.

If I had been able to run I would have rushed, screaming, out into the black mystery of the yard. But I could not run. My knee pained me too much, and I did not dare risk another fall. Not with that silent, breathing thing so close to me.

Inch by inch I crawled past the door. I heard now the click of fingernails against glass. It had found the door too.

Suddenly I rammed my head into a vine climbing over a lattice. I had reached the end of the terrace, and there was no escape from it that way. I drew myself up, and began to feel my way along the lattice. The terrace, I remembered, was about twenty feet wide. It seemed, then, more like twenty yards.

There were steps, then, to the ground. I could not remember if there were two or three. I explored the floor with my toe, trying to locate them. There was no sound of breathing now, but I had the feeling that it was there in the obscurity, almost at my side.

Then it brushed against me—just the feel of a body barely touching me. I froze against the trellis, not breathing, and waited. Whoever it was, it passed by. How it could have avoided hearing my racking heart beats I didn't know. I felt it pass, and I waited, in an agony of suspense.

There was a beating sound against the vines, as if it were patting them, feeling for me. Instantly I shrank back.

Then there was the sound of metal against stone, the sound a shoe-heel makes slipping on tile. A heavy thud followed, as it fell, betrayed by the steps.

Blindly I groped toward the steps.

I heard its voice, soft and whispered, as it swore. Just then I found the steps, and cautiously descended. One, two—three. Gravel was under my foot.

I limped along the path, and struck something hard lying across it. Its leg, I thought, struggling to keep my balance. One more second and I'd be free.

Strong fingers closed around my ankle, dragging me down.

I screamed, then, with sheer terror in my voice. "Help! Help me, somebody!"

The hand jerked at my ankle, and I fell to my hands and knees. Tears sprang into my eyes at the pain in my twisted knee.

"Quiet, you fool!" the voice said sharply, still in that disembodied whisper. I gasped for breath enough to cry out again, and a hot hand closed over my mouth. My ankles were free now, but the hand was pressing against my lips. I tried to open my mouth to bite, and the hand slipped down to my throat. I felt the cruel pressure of two hands now, and the blackness began to swim with little lights like darting balls of flame. In them was one faint steady beam coming closer and closer.

I could not struggle against the strength in those fingers. I thought of Doris Ayers, and the terrible color of her dead face, as my nails tore at the hands choking me.

## *Chapter* XXIV

I CAME out of the dizzy spin slowly, struggling for equilibrium. Lights were revolving over me, and yet gradually focussing— bright bulbs in a frosted shade. Grey walls emerged, and figures hovering near me. They were indistinct but they were there, like the wavering reflections in a rippled pond. Feeling began to return, and I knew I was lying in bed somewhere. One of the figures was a nurse, starched and white, and smiling in a friendly way.

And Al, holding my hand awkwardly and looking like a thundercloud.

"Is she coming around, Miss Kirk?" he asked gruffly, in a voice unlike his own.

"She's coming along nicely," Miss Kirk replied cheerfully. "She'll be all right in a short while now."

I tried to talk, but my throat was dry and swollen. I tried to say, "Al!" but it took all my power. Yet I think he heard me.

"That's the girl, Isabel. Take it easy. Don't talk."

I smiled at him faintly.

And then he was gone, and I closed my eyes, dazzled by the light, and lay there, still spinning like a giddy top, until I drifted to sleep.

Al came to see me early in the morning, almost as soon as I was awake. My throat was still sore and my voice sounded like the raven's croaking "Nevermore." The nurse—not Miss Kirk, but a stolid freckled red-head, with a body solidly composed of motherliness—had at least told me where I was, and that it was the following day, not as I would have assumed, a week later. But she knew nothing more, or refused to tell me, if she did.

Then Al was coming in the door, his arms full of flowers, and his eyes heavy from lack of sleep.

"How long do I have to stay in this damned hospital?" I asked him immediately. "I want to go home."

"I wish," he said, handing the flowers to the nurse, and coming to the bed to look down at me, "I really wish you'd obeyed that impulse to go home right in the beginning. Sometime, my dear, you may decide on it too late."

"Al, be a lamb and tell me what happened."

He pulled up a chair and sat down.

"I will.

"I was on my way to the Emories' to take you home last night, when the blackout started. I got there a few minutes later. Luckily the police cars weren't required to stop. I heard you scream for help, and I got there just as he was choking you to death. I had a flashlight, otherwise I'd never have found you. Isabel, you solved our case for us. But what a way to do it."

"I didn't mean to do it that way, Al. But that mud on Joan's shoes—"

"Don't talk," he ordered.

"All right. But I thought about it. She didn't have time to put the shoes away, but she did put the dress away. It worried me. I thought she'd have taken her shoes off first. I do. Not everybody does, but Joan always did, too. I remembered that. And so—"

"Do you mean to say you figured it out? You didn't just stumble into it by accident?"

"I guess it was stumbling, actually," I confessed. "But, Al, I did see what it meant if she had worn one of Doris' dresses. And Sarah told me one of Doris' dresses was lying on her bed or something. And yet Doris was very neat. She'd have hung it up. So I put two and two together. Joan wore it."

He shook his head wonderingly.

"And you spotted that and blasted as pretty an alibi as I've ever seen."

"But, Al, the point is Joan never knew she was part of an alibi. If she had, she'd never have told me about meeting James at all, and she'd have hidden the shoes. She didn't have much time to, but she'd have tried to do it, somehow."

"And no one else noticed them until you did."

"I *was* right, then, wasn't I?" I asked eagerly. "You see, I couldn't recognize his voice when he chased me last night. He only whispered, and you can't tell about a whisper."

"You were right, all along," said Al, with admiration.

"But why did he try to kill me, Al? How did he know I knew?"

"He was outside the front door when you talked to Sarah. He overheard you through the open peephole. When you came out he hid until you'd gone around back. Then he went inside, and went up to Joan's room. She told him you'd asked questions, and he found out how much she'd told you. He knew then that you suspected. When he went down and saw your car was still there, he knew you were in the grounds somewhere."

"I see." I must have shuddered a little, because Al frowned at me, and started to get up.

"Do you think you'd better rest now?" he asked solicitously.

"Later, Al. Later. I've got to know everything now. It was a carefully planned murder, wasn't it? Not just a spur of the moment thing?"

"Yes, it was. Very carefully planned. He overlooked only one thing—those shoes of Joan's."

"Where is he now?" I asked. He avoided my eye for a moment. "Al, where is he?"

"Isabel, he's dead. I guess you'd find out, if I didn't tell you. I had to—I had to shoot him to save you. There wasn't time for much finesse. He died an hour ago. But we've got his confession. He made a statement before he died."

"Poor Joan!" I said. "She never could choose her men wisely. Frank. And Thorne. And James."

He nodded sympathetically.

"She's really in collapse now," he said. "I don't wonder. But Emory exonerated her completely in his confession.

"Tell me the whole story, Al. Please."

"Well," he said, trying to settle his bulk carefully in the tiny straight chair he was occupying, "according to his statement, he

had counted on Frank's accepting a settlement instead of resort-
ing to action. When he realized that Frank's case was as strong
as it was (he had letters Emory had written that practically tied
up the case) and saw that Frank was vindictive enough to expose
the whole thing, there was only one course open to him: to
eliminate Frank. If he could get away with it, he'd have nothing
further to worry about. He was afraid, however, to kill him at his
own place. Even an alibi can be broken down; in fact, alibis are
suspicious in themselves. And his motive was clear enough to
involve him in spite of himself.

"He decided on boldness to carry him through. It was his way
of doing things. He took Joan boldly; he got her divorce for her
boldly. And he planned Frank's death boldly. He would avoid the
necessity of an alibi by deliberately not having one, but making
the whole murder so open that, on the face of it, no fool would
have committed it that way. It was a risk, of course, but no
greater risk than going to Frank's house to kill him, especially if
it was possible to provide a scapegoat.

"His opportunity came when he overheard his wife make an
appointment to meet Frank here at the house for Thursday night.
He could not take any chances of her suspecting anything, because he could not depend that much on her loyalty. So he arranged to go to to meet his lawyer, and return early. Fortunately
Sherman was busy that night, and he had an excuse to return at
once. If Sherman had actually been there, he'd have left in a few
moments anyway, postponing their talk on some excuse, to a
later time.

"Then, to be sure there was a scapegoat, he allowed Burton
Trent to believe he intended to expose his wife's friendship for
Murdock when the case came to court. Actually, it's possible he
might not ever have done it. But in any case he arranged for Trent
to meet him here about the same time Murdock was here, and
warned him not to come in until he let him in. He wanted Trent
in the grounds but not in the house.

"When he got in that night, he encountered Frank in the upstairs sitting-room at the house and ordered him out of the house.
He sent Joan to her room, knowing that she would obey him, and
then, as he and Frank came downstairs, he shot him, dropping
down on his knee to do it, so the angle of the shot would be upward.

"He wasn't afraid of witnesses. Even if Trent was outside, he
couldn't see the steps from any door or window. The library win-

dows were too high, and the steps weren't in sight from the door. Then he had only to toss the gun out of the library door, and describe the person seen out there.

"Your presence was a surprise and a shock at first, but you played into his hands by telling about seeing the man outside."

"And the gun?" I asked. "Where did he get it?"

"Oh, as we figured, Joan had it among her things. When they packed to go to Reno Doris had helped her, and she had put it in the bag. Emory found it one day and took it. I doubt if Joan even remembered it. Emory, of course, never told her Frank was shot with his own gun. But Doris knew."

"Is that why—?" He nodded.

"One of the reasons. As soon as she learned that, from the Friday evening paper, she suspected him. Doris was no fool. She had put two and two together. She suspected him from the start, but she had no proof until the gun business came out. That was when she telephoned to you, to ask your advice."

"Did Thorne overhear that conversation?" I asked.

"No. He didn't come home with me until later. What happened was this. Doris slipped out of the house, careful not to be seen, and went to wait for you at the circle. She wasn't afraid, because she suspected Emory, and knew he was with me. No one else would have harmed her.

"When Thorne came in, he went up to see Joan. He asked her where Doris was, because he wanted to talk to her at once about taking Elaine away for a few days. Joan told him she'd gone out, so he went out the back way, and down the drive to look for her. He saw her standing at the circle in the street light. He crossed over to her, never dreaming that she knew anything.

"He must have startled her, because she cried out, and told him not to come nearer. She was probably frightened to death, and her fright made it plain to him that she knew the truth. She actually accused him of it. He says she said something like, 'Mr. Emory, I swear I won't tell, only don't hurt me! I won't tell Miss Marsh.' He told her not to be a fool. But she was panicky. 'You're going to kill me so I won't tell,' she said.

"He saw his danger and he did the only thing he could. He strangled her, and hurried back into the house, into Joan's room. He told her he hadn't been able to find Doris, and that it wasn't important. He'd see her later. He was going to come downstairs and talk to me, trying to convince me he hadn't left the house, when Joan, innocently, provided him with a chance to create a perfect alibi.

"She begged him to keep me busy a moment, because James was supposed to meet her downstairs with letters Emory had written to her, which had fallen into Frank's hands."

"I know about those letters," I said. "Go on."

"He promised to keep me busy. And then an inspiration struck him. He told her to slip on one of Miss Ayers' blue dresses before she went down, and to avoid being seen. If anyone did see her they'd believe her to be Doris. In that way the police would not know she had left her room, and James would not be involved.

"Joan, of course, did not realize the true reason for his suggestion. If he could establish a belief that Doris was still alive, and then remain with me until you found her body, his alibi would be complete. And he had James as his scapegoat any time he wanted him."

"How callous!" I cried, in my cracked voice. "Oh, Al, how dreadfully callous!"

"He wanted her to act furtive, of course, which she did. And he rang for drinks so Sarah would be sure to come out of the kitchen, and yet return to it in time to see Joan, in Doris' dress, slip out. In a dim light it would be easy to mistake one for the other. They were about the same build, with dark hair. And Doris' blue dresses were her constant attire, so much so that anyone seeing such a dress would assume Doris was wearing it."

"You know, Joan really gave it all away to me," I put in, "when she said that Doris had come to tell her she was going out, wearing her hat. Whatever became of the hat?"

"Emory knocked it off her head when he choked her. He picked it up, and carried it back into the house. He hung it in Doris' closet as he came up."

\* \* \*

That, really, was the whole story. There were one or two points that weren't cleared up for a while, but they too, were settled in the days that followed. Burton Trent's hundred thousand dollars, for example. Frank had locked the cash and securities in a tin box he had in the house, for valuables. When James heard of Frank's death that night, he had turned over the letters and other papers belonging to Frank. But the cash box he had hidden, because Joan's letters were inside it. He was absolutely astonished when he opened it the next day and found the money. He saw then no need to broadcast the fact that it was there. He simply hid it when the police searched his place, by burying it in a window box under some geraniums. As for the letter to the lawyer, Post, with Burton's note from Frank, that had never been mailed. Frank had handed it to James to drop in a mail box for him, and James had simply forgotten it. He'd left it in his car, tucked under the sun shade. Later, when he found the money, he opened the letter and discovered where the money had come from. He destroyed the note at once, in hopes that Burton would not have any proof then that he had paid it to Frank.

There was one other thing that puzzled me, especially after we found that James actually had gone to the movies Thursday. I wanted to know who Burton had seen looking in the peephole of the front door of the Emory house. It was a long time before we knew. It turned out to be one of those odd, irrelevant things that can, at times, be so confusing. That Thursday night the Emories' neighbors had been having guests in for bridge. One of them had mistaken the house, and had gone to the Emories' door. The peephole was open and he had looked in.

I myself did not remain in the hospital long. Twenty-four hours in there was all I could take, and I came home in spite of protesting nurses, screaming doctors, and an Al who was firm, but not quite firm enough.

He called the first evening I was back, and treated me as if I were in the midst of a long convalescence. Not that it wasn't pleasant to be fussed over a little.

"But, Isabel, haven't you learned your lesson?" he asked as we both sat before an open fire in my den.

He knelt beside my chair like a big overgrown boy, and put his arms around me.

"I'd have killed anyone that night if I'd seen them hurting you. I—I guess I can't take shocks like that, my dear."

I drew closer to him.

"You know how I feel," he said. "I don't have to tell you again. I've said all I could. It's just up to you now."

I looked around the den, at the warm fire, and at Al, comfortingly there where I wanted him; where, I knew, I would always want him.

There was no hesitation any longer, no doubt in my mind.

"Isabel, will you stop being a silly spinster, and marry me?"

Well, after all, what could I say to that but what I did?